Cover Design: Missy Walker

Editor: Swish Design & Editing

To my readers—thank you for picking up this book. I promise it's better than my grocery list, and it has way more drama.

SCARRED HEART

ELITE MEN OF LOS ANGELES #1

MISSY WALKER

1

SPENCER

"Ohh... shi-it... so close..." The nameless blonde tossed her hair to the side so she could look at me over her shoulder. "Harder," she whispered, meeting me thrust for thrust.

If there was one thing I believed in, it was giving a lady what she wanted. My grip on her hips tightened so I could hold her in place before pounding into her in sharp, deep strokes that left her clenching around my dick while she bit her lip to silence a moan.

This was nothing. A distraction, a little fun. Short-lived, but then bathroom sex generally had to be, especially when it took place in a public bathroom at a Hollywood industry event.

Burying myself balls deep, she gripped the marble, her legs trembling as she tipped over the edge, causing my orgasm to follow. Then I slipped out of her and tossed the condom, tucking myself into my boxer briefs. "Thanks for that," I offered dryly, zipping my pants.

"Mmm... thank *you*." The woman purred like a cat, her red nails trailing down my chest after she righted herself and flicked my silk tie in a gesture that was probably supposed to be playful. As far as I was concerned, she'd already worn out her welcome. "We should try that again sometime. Maybe someplace a little more private. Not that this wasn't incredible," she added.

Fucking her while she leaned over the sink was hardly incredible, but then I couldn't speak for her prior experience. For all I knew, I was the best she'd ever had. "I'd better get back out there," I told her, ignoring the way her face fell when I avoided the topic of getting together again. One last look in the mirror confirmed everything was in place before I offered a brief smile and headed for the door. "Give me a minute before following." I didn't bother to stick around to hear if she said anything more. It didn't matter.

After all, I was under strict orders not to fuck

around with any of the women at this event. My best friend, Lex Landry, had invited me to the awards ceremony and luncheon honoring his father. Being the son of a legendary studio mogul meant sitting through boring events. I was allowed to alleviate the boredom, but only if I promised to leave the young actresses alone.

His family studio, handed down from grandfather to father and soon to son, had sat at the top of the Hollywood heap for decades. There wasn't an actress in town who wouldn't kill for a role in one of the films they produced. While Lex had never participated in that whole casting couch bullshit, rumors could be vicious. The slightest hint of that swirling around him might be more than enough to shift public perception.

The coast was clear when I stepped out. Lex was nowhere in sight. Straightening my suit jacket, I scanned the banquet room for him, wondering if he needed a wingman to free him from a dull conversation.

Instead of finding him, I swore I saw a ghost.

For one breathless moment, my heart stopped beating—the reaction that resulted from a sudden shock. It couldn't be *her* weaving her way through the crowd with a tall, shapely goddess following close behind. It wasn't possible.

A scream rang out in my head as sharp and clear as the night I heard it coming from the girl in the passenger seat—shrill, terror-filled, with the power to lift the hair on the back of my neck.

Other memories flooded back, overlapping chaotically, reflecting the chaos of that terrible night. The crunch of metal, the shattering of glass. The terrifying, profound silence in the moments after we came to a violent stop when I looked to my right and found a nightmare come to life.

So much blood. I didn't know people had that much blood in them. She can't be alive. But she can't be dead.

The purr of the women exiting the bathroom behind me pulled me back to the present, but she wasn't the blonde who'd taken my mind hostage. "Will I see you again?" the stranger asked. I never did get her name. If I had, I would've forgotten it the second I thought I saw the woman who'd changed the course of my life.

"I don't think so," I murmured without glancing at the nameless blonde, already on my way to where I would've sworn I saw her.

Rowan.

A name I hadn't spoken aloud in years, one which only existed in my memory now.

Get it together. I was more tense now than I'd been before sneaking off to that rather dirty bathroom with one of the event staff. Why the hell would memories of Rowan haunt me now? I hadn't thought about her in years, a deliberate avoidance at first that became easier as time went on.

"Wake up. You have to wake up!" Fuck, so many things could race through a person's mind all at once. That scream of hers. The sound someone made when they knew they were about to die, only *she couldn't be dead.*

"There you are." Lex's warm, jovial voice startled me out of the nightmare that insisted on wrapping itself around me. Of course, I hadn't seen her. This town was overflowing with beautiful blondes.

"Here I am," I replied. "Sorry if I left you hanging."

"I figured I'd find you screwing a starlet in the bathroom," he joked, his gaze moving over the room.

"I wouldn't do that." And I hadn't. I was true to my word. "If anything, this is a little boring. I thought these big industry parties evolved into orgies."

"So that's why you were so quick to accept my invitation." He lifted his drink to acknowledge an old man who waved across the room. "Sorry. wrong decade. Though I bet that old geezer over there could tell you a few stories."

What a shame, considering the quality of the women around us. Not only were they gorgeous, but they were willing. Almost hungry. I knew the look in their eyes and the determination written across their perfect faces. Somebody needed to tell them not to smile so hard. It looked forced. If there was one skill an actress needed, it was the ability to look sincere.

But this wasn't a set, and we weren't making a movie. It didn't matter. Hollywood wasn't known for realism. Every event was an opportunity to make a good impression on a director, agent, or executive, and an event such as the one my best friend had roped me into attending was no exception.

Sinking into a chair along the room's periphery, I could at least relax my facial muscles. It was different in the Hamptons last weekend at the wedding where I could genuinely be glad for the couple getting married. Besides, it was good to see my colleague, Miles Young, looking at peace for a little while despite everything going on around us.

Here, things were the complete opposite—a

façade I wouldn't subject myself to if it weren't for my best friend.

Lex only chuckled, sipping his whiskey. This was his world. He'd grown up in his dad's office, hanging around the studio after school and during summer breaks. After lifting a hand to acknowledge a pair of suited executives a few tables away from ours, he said, "You needed an excuse to get out for a little while. Relax, have another drink, take a breath. Work will be there later."

"Who said I was thinking about work?" I asked, even as my thoughts returned to the phone in my pocket. It hadn't buzzed with an incoming message, yet my fingers twitched out of a need to check the damn thing. Again.

He snorted, giving me the sort of look one friend gave another after a decade of joint shenanigans. "Call me psychic."

A redhead in a pantsuit spotted me as she walked past with a glass of wine in one hand and her phone in the other. Though she was in the middle of a conversation, our eyes locked, and her gaze softened. I knew that look—the spark of interest as she took me in.

What a shame my phone buzzed when it did. I grabbed it and pulled it out, my heart pounding in expectation. The redhead might as well have not existed as I skimmed a text from one of my contacts back on the East Coast. In the week since Rose Goldsmith's store had all but burned to the ground, the only thing anyone knew for sure was the presence of an accelerant at the scene. Arson.

"How many times are you gonna do that?" Lex asked, eyeing my phone once I placed it face down on the table. "Your friends in New York are working on it. There's nothing that piece of shit Damian Fields can do to stop your patent from being approved."

Easy for him to say. He hadn't stood back and watched with a sinking heart while scorched timbers fell onto smoking ruins. He hadn't heard the heartbroken weeping from the girls whose bridal gowns had gone up in flames. There hadn't been a question in my mind of how the fire had started and who was behind it. Arson was one of Damian's go-to methods for getting rid of competitors. I'd only waited for the initial report to confirm my suspicions.

Lex finished off his drink, then held up his glass to a passing server, signaling for a refill. "It's almost funny seeing all the love you're getting online."

"All the love *Miles* is getting," I corrected. He would be in Hawaii by now, living it up with his new wife while I did my best to keep things together on this side of the Pacific. Somehow, I doubted Aria had his full attention, especially now that Damian's team had begun to leak information about Miles' past, including a bar fight that had resulted in his opponent being paralyzed by a traumatic brain injury.

Lucian Diamond, one of Miles' friends and heir to a media empire, worked with his girlfriend, Ivy, and their digital team to flood the internet with positive stories. Photos from the lavish wedding were interspersed with tales recounting the stress of finding last-minute replacements for the bridal party's attire. They worked toward drumming up sympathy and admiration to drown out what painted him in a negative light.

I swirled the ice in my glass, seething, pushing it as deep down as I could for the sake of keeping up appearances. Not for my sake but for Lex, whose father was one of the recipients of the humanitarian award presented earlier this afternoon.

What would it have been like having a father worth looking up to? From the time I was barely old enough to count to ten, bystanders had assumed I would take the reins and oversee the family's shipping empire. As if I'd want to play any part in the way Dad encouraged exploitation, cost cutting, conveniently ignoring regulations to increase profits.

In contrast, Alexander Landry was currently in the center of a group of admirers scrambling to get his attention like a bunch of neglected children, hoping Daddy would tell them they were his favorite. He might not have noticed the way they tried to claw each other out of the way, but I did, and it made me laugh to myself.

Lex noticed, snickering. "Don't ever let him try to fool you," he muttered as he watched the worship people heaped on his old man. "He loves it. He only acts like it gets on his nerves, the way they kiss his ass."

"What about you?" I asked. "Do you hate having your ass kissed?"

"Me?" He shrugged blithely. "Why bother acting? What's the point of owning a studio if you can't enjoy the perks of the position?"

"Careful," I warned, not joking anymore. "That sounds a hell of a lot like the sort of shit the studio heads said back in his early days." They probably said much worse than that.

He scoffed before accepting a fresh drink. "A bunch of old pricks who couldn't get laid any other way. Everybody knows Sunset Pictures would never get mixed up in some vile shit like that."

They were one in a million, then. I would've told him so, but his father's assistant came over to murmur something in Lex's ear. My thoughts wandered, and my gaze followed suit, drifting over the clusters of people socializing and networking rather than eating the lunch provided to us.

There! It's her! I was on my feet in an instant, scanning the room in search of the blonde who looked so much like my past. "Who did you spot?" Lex asked once he noticed me gazing over the heads of countless strangers.

Where the fuck had she gone?

"Nobody." I was too stressed. That was the problem. My overwrought brain was going haywire while my team worked their fingers to the bone in hopes of completing the patent application and getting it out before Damian's team could do the same. We had no way of knowing exactly how far along they were in the application process. I only knew I'd lost two team members in the past year who'd ended up as employees of FieldCo not long after.

How much had he offered them? How much did a person's professional integrity go for nowadays? No doubt he would've guaranteed legal representation if we chose to sue, but then there was no proof they'd sold our company's secrets to him. Not yet, anyway.

"Oh, for fuck's sake." Lex rolled his eyes dramatically when I looked his way. "What is she doing here? How would somebody like her get in?"

"Who?" I followed the direction of his gaze to find a girl with auburn hair and arms full of bangles chatting with a few women. The word 'bohemian' came to mind. She was wearing Birkenstocks, for Christ's sake.

"Summer Strawbridge." His nose wrinkled like the name smelled foul. "A wannabe director with a shitty attitude. I hope she doesn't think she'll get work here."

I didn't answer. I couldn't. Because once Summer drifted away, I caught sight of the woman she'd been chatting with—a tall, willowy brunette.

And Rowan.

As beautiful as ever, she tucked a strand of golden hair behind her ear and let her fingertips trace her earlobe so she could fidget with her earring —a gesture I would've recognized anywhere a decade after I'd last seen it.

So much came back. Not only that tragic night but the good times. When I took her to our vacation house in Malibu and promised to teach her to surf. It hadn't gone well, considering we couldn't stop screwing around in the surf long enough to focus. Riding the Ferris wheel on the Santa Monica Pier, laughing as she squealed when we got stuck at the top. And how had she paid me back for laughing? By letting me walk around the busy pier for at least an hour with melted ice cream on my chin, oblivious. I could hear her laughter over my pounding heart.

"Hello?" Lex snapped his fingers in front of my face.

I slapped his hand away without thinking about it, still staring at the blonde who'd stepped out of my past into the present. *Look at me, dammit.* I needed her to see me but would be damned if I begged for her attention.

"What the hell are you... *oh.*" There was laughter in my friend's voice once he followed the direction of my gaze. "I know that look. You spotted somebody."

I nodded, only half hearing him. Where the hell had she gone? The girl had disappeared off the face of the earth only to show up at the least likely moment. There were times when I had actually questioned whether she existed at all. Otherwise, why had it been so easy for her to vanish from my life?

"As always, you have a good eye," Lex mused.

His laughter barely registered in my awareness. I was too focused on her, following her every movement, my heart jumping every time she turned her head far enough for me to get a glimpse of her profile. Her nose was different, I realized, and for some reason, the realization left me with a sinking sensation. The girl I knew had one of those perky ski-jump noses. She'd sworn it was natural, that she hadn't had any work done, though people used to ask her about it all the time, wondering which plastic surgeon she'd used.

Still, I couldn't take my eyes off her. "Do you know who she is?" I asked as she and the brunette sat at an otherwise empty table. Why was I asking? Maybe I didn't want to believe it. Maybe it was easier back when I imagined her slipping out of the world the way she had slipped out of my life. Like we never mattered.

Or like we had stopped mattering because of me. That was the answer, it had always been. I'd carried it with me all these years. One of those deep-seated beliefs a man doesn't have to devote conscious thought to. I didn't have to give any prolonged thought to gravity, but the evidence of it was around me all the time.

"Yeah, I've seen her around town. She might be

working with a girl who signed onto that new action movie we're looking to release next summer." Lex drummed his fingers along the table. "An entertainment lawyer. She focuses on young actresses, making sure they don't get taken advantage of when they sign a contract."

A lawyer? It was not the way I remembered things, but then a lot of water had passed under the bridge. I was hardly the person I used to be when we were together. Why wouldn't she have changed?

"Commendable," he mused, though he sounded bored when he said it. I understood why when he continued, "She's a real pain-in-the-ass ball-buster when she puts her mind to it. Rumor has it she used to be an actress, so she knows what to look out for."

Bingo. The word actress was all I needed to hear. "Is her name Rowan?" I asked, knowing the answer but needing confirmation as my heart threatened to smash through my chest.

He snapped his fingers in a eureka moment. "It is. Rowan McNulty? I think that's it."

I knew her as Rowan Leslie. Stupid ass. It was clearly a stage name she came up with for her acting career. People did it all the time. No wonder I couldn't find her when I tried. *After...*

"Where are you going?" Lex asked when I stood

and buttoned my suit jacket before downing what was left of my tequila.

"Where do you think?" I countered, dropping my phone into my pocket. It could have rung with a call from my office or Damian Fields himself, and I would've ignored it. Nodding in Rowan's direction, I said, "You're going to introduce me."

"Since when am I your wingman?" he asked with a laugh.

It wasn't about that, but there was no time to explain. I wouldn't have known where to begin. He didn't know about her. Almost no one did. "Would you do this without complaining?" I muttered while I waited for him to stop bitching and get off his ass. He did, though he continued grumbling.

Not that it mattered when my good sense battled it out in my head with questions more than a decade old. It would've been smarter to leave her alone. To forget I saw her and let her go on with her life.

2

ROWAN

"You're doing fine." I gave my latest client the most reassuring smile I could manage. The poor kid was shaking like a leaf and reminding me of hell a lot of myself around a decade ago. "Just be natural. Don't try too hard to impress anybody."

"That's easy for you to say," she reminded me with a tight little laugh. Penny Hargrove, all five feet ten inches of her, with a waterfall of inky hair that hung partway over her face. I used to wear my hair that way, then I said fuck it and cut it off. "You're not the one trying to make a good impression on everybody in case somebody decides to give you a chance."

Her hands trembled as she ran them over her

thighs. The pale peach dress she wore played up her delicate complexion and big green eyes. I had recommended it with that in mind. "Remember what I told you when we first met? Do you remember when you first walked into my office? I told you why I do what I do. I remember what it was like."

There it was, that quick, almost imperceptible glance. Her eyes shifted for just a second before darting away, but it was enough. I followed her gaze to the mirror, to the reflection I no longer recognized. I couldn't ignore it, but after ten years and a lot of fading, the scars weren't as noticeable as they once were.

There was a time when my entire world revolved around them. Were they getting fainter yet? Was there another brand of makeup that would cover them better? A hairstyle that would conceal them?

I was used to that glance and the obvious disbelief that went along with it. She was young, barely off the bus from her little no-name town in the Midwest. There were so many like her in a town practically built upon the discarded dreams of bright, beautiful young women. Hell, she didn't even have an agent yet. It was because of that I took her on as a client. She might as well have been wearing a

Little Red Riding Hood costume, walking through the big, scary woods while predators and cheats lurked around every corner, wondering how to take advantage of her.

"Remember," I told her, glossing over the pointed look at my scars. "You're here to make an impression. Nobody is holding a gun to your head. All you need to do is smile."

"Maybe I can talk with Mr. Landry?" She rolled her shoulders back, lifting her chin, scanning the room. "I could thank him for putting me in the movie and make sure he knows how seriously I'm going to take the job." The wide-eyed kid looked and sounded almost painfully sincere.

"There's no need." Her face fell a little like I popped her balloon. The girl needed an agent. Somebody to give her this sort of advice since mine was only supposed to be that of the legal variety.

"You're not the first actress who thought they may be able to get away with that," I explained. "Trust me. Pros like him see straight through it. It might end up doing more harm than good if he thinks you're a fake or a kiss-ass."

I was starting to wish I had never mentioned this event while studying the contract she'd received from the studio. I had looked at the invitation as a professional courtesy and was on the fence about whether or not I wanted to go in the first place. When she found out I was invited, she had done everything short of standing on her head to get me to add her as my guest. There were other things I could be doing that I would've enjoyed more than wearing an empty smile and posing for a photo when appropriate.

Not that I was in a position to be a snob about any of it. My practice was barely two years old, and it had only been within the last quarter that I'd been in a position to take on a third paralegal. It was time to start thinking seriously about expansion. That meant showing my face at award lunches and other events.

"Oh my God." Something over my shoulder caught Penny's eye. Her already fair skin went white as a sheet. "He's coming this way. Lex Landry. I can't breathe."

"Relax," I whispered, caught between a tiny bit of irritation and the impulse to laugh at her. She had already signed on to do a brainless action movie with the studio. The time to impress him and his dad and the other big shots would come once filming started.

I turned slightly to ask a server for a glass of

chardonnay, giving me a glimpse of the man Penny was hyperventilating over. From the corner of my eye, I could just make out the sight of him cutting through the crowd. All in all, he wasn't a bad guy. At least, I had never heard anything about him beyond rumors of being a womanizer, which was nothing special in this town. So long as the women consented and they weren't coerced in any way, it was none of my business.

"Don't be too eager," I warned, looking down at the floor and composing myself the way I hoped she was. She wasn't my only client who'd signed on to make movies at his studio. I needed to maintain a warm relationship. My client roster was healthy, but I was in no position to take chances.

"Mr. Landry. It's so nice to see you." Gone was the nervous, fidgeting girl. Now she was a sophisticated, worldly woman who oozed charm and confidence once Lex reached us. "Congratulations to your father. I haven't been in town long, but I know what an honor this award is." The girl was smooth. If she were half as convincing in front of a camera, there was a solid career ahead of her.

Lex stood a step behind me, chuckling. "Thank you. Forgive me, but I'm no good with names,

Miss..." Only a guy in his position would cut to the chase like that.

"Penny Hargrove," she purred. Meanwhile, I accepted a glass of ice-cold wine once it reached me and took a long sip, pretending I wasn't listening to every word. Let her make her impression.

A second male voice rang out over my right shoulder, softer than Lex's. "You look like somebody I used to know."

That voice. Rich, deep, like warm honey rolling down my body, coating me in sweetness. The last voice I thought I'd ever hear again. The world stopped for a second. The room went silent or was that my heartbeat drowning out everything else?

Suddenly, I was twenty again, with my entire life ahead of me and nothing but hope and dreams to sustain me. Images flashed across my mind's eye, covering the six months Spencer Collins was part of my life. Everything he'd shown me. A world I would never have known if it hadn't been for him.

What a shame it wasn't enough to make up for everything that came after.

My mind caught up to reality, and everything came rushing back. When I looked up, stunned, my head spun, and goose bumps covered my skin. The sight of those icy blue eyes made my heart skip a beat.

It's like something out of a movie.

Amazing, the things that will go through a person's head at a moment like this. Confronted with the man who'd changed the course of my life. Somebody I told myself it was better not to see since the past was the past. I didn't need him.

Yet, there he was in front of me, the last person I ever expected to set eyes on again, especially at an event like this, with half the town in attendance to honor one of the few men in the industry with no skeletons in the closet. Sometimes, that was more than enough to earn accolades. There were too many horror stories in this business, enough to outweigh the dreams of fame and fortune.

Fame and fortune I had once dreamed of.

Fame and fortune stolen from me by the man now invading my space, destroying my composure.

My hand closed tighter around the stem of my wine glass, and my jaw ached from clenching my teeth as the past and present collided in my head.

"Rowan McNulty, right?" He was playing dumb, but it didn't matter to my pounding heart. No one had ever said my name the way Spencer did. Any hope of my overworked mind pretending I was imagining things was lost when I heard it spoken in a voice that still haunted my dreams sometimes. A voice that, at one time, I would have done anything to hear.

"That's my name," I somehow managed to choke out while holding his gaze. How I could speak while staring at him was a mystery I couldn't afford to investigate. He had barely aged a day, and the changes time had brought on only made him more handsome.

"Do we know each other?" His head tipped to the side, blue eyes tracing a path over my body. Damn my nipples for tightening the way they did while my heart beat faster and my mouth went dry. Damn for doing this to me. Looking me up and down like I was a prize heifer after vanishing off the face of the planet and abandoning me. Pretending not to remember me when we both knew he did. What gave him the right?

"This is a small town," I pointed out. "It only feels big." It was a miracle I could force out a single word with my jaw so tightly clenched.

How? Where had he come from? For years, I told myself he was gone, out of my life, and good riddance. I didn't need him. I never had. I only thought I did.

"I know." He snapped his fingers, his mouth twisting into a smirk that confirmed he was playing a game. "You went by a different name when we knew each other. Rowan Leslie, wasn't it?"

Nobody had called me that in years. "You have a good memory," I murmured, wearing a thin smile. Now that the shock started to clear up, something else took its place that turned my bewilderment into something harder. "I wouldn't have expected anyone to remember that. It's been such a long time."

"It has." He still had the power to look straight through me and see what was inside. I wanted to escape his perceptive gaze before he saw more than I wanted to reveal. Every instinct told me to leave, to go, to put this behind me and not turn back.

I couldn't afford this.

I couldn't survive him.

I barely survived the first time.

"Let's see how fast this baby can really go." I blinked rapidly, trying to push the memory of his teasing invitation aside. That was then. This was now. Only the past and present had a funny way of overlapping and getting all mixed up.

Looking at him, I saw the polished man before me and the arrogant, insolent, wild thing he used to be. I saw everything about him that had, for some reason, turned me into a brainless, careless idiot.

"That's what stage names are for," I concluded with a shrug. "Anyway, that was another lifetime."

"Yes, it was." His jaw ticked, and his nostrils flared. I had to be imagining this, or did he have the audacity to look angry? He certainly didn't look at me like an old friend. I was a bug he wanted to squash.

He wasn't the only one with the skill to see through people.

"Anyway..." Lex cleared his throat, and dammit, I had almost forgotten he was standing there. I had forgotten Penny too. Everything else had ceased to exist.

The man still had a strange power over me.

I turned my full attention onto Lex. "It's nice to see so many people in attendance in your dad's honor," I offered, shaking his hand. "He looked great up there while giving his speech. What's it like, inheriting such fantastic genes?"

His broad shoulders shook when he laughed. "If I'm in half his shape once I reach that age, I'll be the luckiest bastard alive."

Meanwhile, Spencer stared holes through me while I pretended not to care. What was he doing here? I wanted to ask. There were so many things I wanted to ask. For the time being, I settled for running a hand through my long bob, deliberately revealing the scar running along my temple and halfway down the side of my face. He wanted to stare at me? Might as well give him a look at what he hadn't bothered to see before now.

"Once you sign this contract, you forfeit your ability to contact Mr. Collins ever again. For any reason."

All of a sudden, I was in a hospital bed, staring up through a fog of pain and heartache at a man in black who loomed over me with a contract in one hand. *"You will have the money you need to finance a fresh start."*

I had signed away the right to ask Spencer a damn thing ever again. At the time, it had seemed like the only thing to do. Flailing around in the middle of a stormy sea with nothing to grab onto, here was a man offering security, if nothing else.

Just then, security was one thing I was short on.

Spencer had run away from me like the cowardly child he was, and now he had the nerve to stare daggers at me. When I took the chance to glance his way, the intensity in his gaze sent a cold shiver down my spine.

Ten years. No, eleven. Where had he been?

"My friend Spencer is in the middle of patenting a new piece of technology, in fact." Lex gestured toward Spencer with his drink, unaware of the icy tension that hung between us. "Before long, his company will be the new Apple."

"Please, nobody quote me as saying that," Spencer quipped. Penny giggled and—*fuck me*—fluttered her eyelashes at him. My nails dug into my palm as I fought the urge to drag her from the ballroom by her hair. He had already destroyed my dreams. I'd be damned if I let him do it to her.

"Lex?" Alexander Landry, Sr. waved his son over from halfway across the room, motioning toward a handful of photographers.

Lex let out another charming little chuckle while shrugging. "Duty calls. Penny, want me to introduce you? I'm sure he'd be happy to meet an up-and-coming star like you."

Penny nodded and only blurted out a tiny giggle, her wide eyes meeting mine. I gave her a slight nod of encouragement and watched her fall in step beside the studio executive who'd left me standing alone with Spencer.

"Rowan." He stepped up closer, almost overwhelming me with his presence. There was so much of him. He was too tall, too commanding, too intense. It was still an intoxicating combination. "I need to speak with you about something very important. Crucial."

"After all this time?" I asked, faking the insolence I wished was real. "I can't imagine what it might be."

"Give me thirty minutes over drinks tonight," he insisted. His nerve made my head snap back, but he ignored it. He was good at ignoring what was inconvenient. "I promise it'll be worth the time. And if you don't think I'll have Lex look up your number for me—"

I'd heard enough. Pinching the bridge of my nose, I whispered, "Fine, fine." I would hate myself for this. I was sure of it. He didn't deserve a minute of my time after forcing me into signing that stupid contract I was too naïve and immature to understand.

But that contract, along with the pain that had come before it, placed my feet on the path I now walked. I couldn't pretend it was all bad.

The things we tell ourselves when we need an excuse to see a man one more time.

His jaw tightened as he nodded, looking me up and down one more time, grunting out, "Bar Nineteen12. Eight o'clock."

And then he was gone, cutting through the

crowd like a hot knife through soft butter. I reached out blindly, grabbing for the back of the closest chair to support myself now that the adrenaline that had kept me upright drained from my system. His broad back retreated, the crowd swallowing him, but I continued staring in that direction for what felt like forever.

The bastard wanted to see me tonight and according to him, it was crucial.

Had he waited more than ten years to apologize for almost killing me? Or did he want to apologize for buying my silence like the spoiled coward he was?

One thing was for sure. I wouldn't miss this appointment for the world.

3

——————

SPENCER

Life could be a bad fucking joke sometimes. A day might begin with doing a favor for a friend, but then it ended with a man's past being thrown in his face.

It was a quarter to eight, and Rowan had yet to show herself, leaving me waiting in a corner booth that faced the room. When she arrived—and she would—I wanted to know. I wanted to watch her walk toward me, read her body language and expression as well as prepare myself somehow since her appearance today had knocked me off a cliff and sent me into a freefall.

I hadn't thought about her. I was too busy thinking about Miles, about his mistakes and how they might come back to haunt us. Rowan, on the other hand? Maybe it was easier to imagine her as a ghost. The ghost she had transformed herself into with no help from me.

Of all the people to get in the way of this deal going through, I had overlooked the one who may tank my entire life, my reputation, everything I had broken my back to build over the past decade. I was supposed to be on top of this shit, a step ahead of Damian. How could I have forgotten her?

You forced yourself to forget.

I would need a hell of a lot more than a single drink to ease the pressure in my head. It had taken two years on the other side of the world, but I had eventually gotten her out of my system. The job my old man had forced me into turned out to be the best thing for me. I'd turned into a serious person, someone miles away from the arrogant, ignorant child I used to be. A trip that had started off as a way of getting me out of the country and out of the lime-light had been my saving grace.

She had answered one question today, anyway—why I hadn't been able to find her. I had only ever known her as the person she wanted to be. Rowan Leslie, ingenue, the starlet waiting in the wings for her big break. No wonder I hadn't quite recognized her at first. It must have taken serious plastic surgery to undo the damage I'd caused.

"*Spencer!*" That high-pitched scream. Like something from an animal. Full of terror. Capable of freezing my guts years later.

And then everything else. The jarring crash. The shattering of glass and crunching of metal. Sirens. Flashing lights.

Silence from the passenger's seat.

I may have been sitting in a comfortable, elegant lounge, but my memory was a different story. In my head, I was in a brightly lit, noisy hospital hallway.

Blood pounded in my ears, louder than the hiss of the fluorescent lights above, as I stood just outside the ER doors. My legs felt like jelly, the sterile scent of antiseptic clinging to my skin, suffocating me. She was in bad shape when they rushed her to the hospital, bad enough that they kept me away while they worked on her. The moment they whisked her away, the color drained from the world, replaced by an agonizing blur of whites and grays. Nurses and doctors had all but shoved me out of the way, their voices a rush of medical jargon I couldn't decipher.

Still, after several hours, I had no answers, but Dad's lawyer tracked me down, advising me to get the hell out of there. To go home and pretend I had nothing to do with the crash.

When dawn finally broke, I bolted through the hospital's sliding doors, desperate. My breath caught in my throat when I saw her bed—empty. Not even the crumpled sheets were left behind. Panic clawed at my chest. The whir of wheels on linoleum blurred into a dizzying chaos as I darted around, my feet moving too fast to keep up with my frantic thoughts.

"Where is she?" My voice cracked, barely audible above the hum of machines. The nurse at the desk didn't look up, flipping through paperwork.

"Transferred."

Transferred? The word slammed into me, sending my heart plummeting. "To where? Where did they take her?" The faces around me blurred, a sea of blank expressions as if no one even noticed my world collapsing.

"We only know she was taken to another hospital," one of the nurses at the desk said with a short, empty shrug. And that was it.

My thumb hovered over her name on the screen, my pulse racing in sync with the ringing. One ring. Two rings. No answer. The silence was crushing, more deafening than if she'd yelled. I stared at the phone, expecting the call to disconnect any second. Maybe she blocked me. Hell, I would've done the same if I were her.

I dragged a hand through my hair, the tension coiled in my chest tightening. The air felt thick as I made my way back to the car, the streetlights flickering in the early evening dusk. I got in, but even the hum of the engine couldn't cut through the dead quiet that settled over me. It pressed in, suffocating, relentless.

Three days. Three long, silent days where the phone never lit up with her name, no angry texts, no desperate calls. Just... nothing.

When I finally worked up the nerve to go to her place, my gut twisted the moment I spotted the moving van outside. The front door stood open, the last rays of daylight casting long shadows over the boxes being carried out. I stopped, frozen at the edge of the sidewalk. Every thud of a box hitting the floor was a punch to the gut.

She was leaving. Moving on without me. And I had no one to blame but myself.

I cringed now at the memory of offering the moving crew an eye-popping amount of money to tell me where they were going with Rowan's things. At the time, I'd almost exploded in rage when they refused and then threatened to call the cops if I trailed them.

Fuck, I had almost wanted them to. For the first

time in my twenty-two years, I'd felt sorry for something I did. I wanted to be punished.

That was the one thing that stuck with me, that I wished I might have told her if she'd given me the chance. I couldn't blame her for turning her back on me after what I had done. I couldn't ask for forgiveness. I had no right to it. I had destroyed her life, killed her dreams, left her with a future that in no way resembled the one she'd been working toward.

Things didn't look so destroyed now, considering what I'd observed earlier. She had found a way to turn everything around and build something for herself. Somehow, I doubted her current success meant I was off the hook for my part in the pivot she'd been forced to perform.

A wry grin tipped the corners of my mouth as I signaled for another tequila. It was a few minutes until eight, but I wasn't worried. She'd show up. And if she didn't, there wouldn't be any hiding from me this time. I could find her, or else I would forfeit any hope of a decent night's sleep until I knew for sure there was no hit coming out against me.

My eyes roamed lazily across the room, scanning the dimly lit lounge, drifting from table to table. Then, they shifted, almost of their own accord, snapping to the hostess stand, and there she was. My entire focus narrowed until all I saw was her golden hair, a beacon in the dimly lit lounge. I had to be out of my mind—that was the only explanation for my rapid pulse and shortened breath.

I imagined destroying her beauty for good like she ended up as some grotesque monster because I took a blind curve without easing up on the gas pedal. If anything, she was more beautiful than I remembered. The way she wore her hair, parted in the middle and hanging straight, meant most of her thin scar was covered. Anyone looking up from their table as she approached would see a blonde, blue-eyed, porcelain skin goddess.

My mouth went dry as I stood, waiting for her to slide into the high-backed leather booth. It was a semicircular shape, but rather than meet me in the middle, she sat close to the end. Like she wanted to hedge her bets in case a quick escape was necessary.

"Thank you for meeting me," I offered, noting her chilly attitude.

She hardly looked at me as she settled in with a sigh. "You didn't give me much of a choice." Rolling her eyes, she added, "Threatening to get my number from Lex Landry. You move in different circles than you used to."

"That makes two of us." Everything about her

was polished, from her glossy hair to the Birkin bag she carried over one shoulder and the stilettos she walked in like they were tennis shoes. The girl I used to know was gone.

I wanted to get to know the woman now. The idea sparked hunger deep in my core, so sudden and intense it shocked me before I pushed it down. *Jerk off later. Business now.* "You look great. Professional." Fuck me, what kind of line was that? I'd have any other woman eating from the palm of my hand by now.

This was not any other woman.

Her smile was weak. "Thank you."

"I was impressed seeing you today," I added. "You've made a good name for yourself from what I hear."

Her head tipped to the side. "You know, you don't have to compliment me. I don't need you to make me feel like things aren't so bad."

A server dropped by long enough for Rowan to order a glass of wine while I reconsidered my plan of attack. She was too sharp to fall for compliments, and she wasn't shy about referring to the accident and any guilt I might feel.

"That's not what I was doing," I insisted once we were on our own again.

"I'm just saying, I know where this is coming from, and I don't need to hear it." A smug grin tipped her mouth. "I'm fine. My life has gone well."

For the sake of keeping things positive, I forced myself to overlook the smugness. "I'm glad to hear it. Tell me about your practice."

"You don't really want to know about my practice, do you?"

Her deadpan delivery brought me up short. So much for pleasantries. "How can you say that?"

"Can we cut the bullshit for a minute?" Her wine arrived, but she left it untouched, folding her slim arms on the table. "Why did you want me to come here tonight? It's been eleven years, and somehow fate put us together in the same room, and you tell me there's something important we have to talk about. No, I think the word you used was *crucial*. It was crucial that we have a drink tonight. Why? To catch up? Respectfully, I have other things to do." She lifted her glass and took a sip, her gaze unflinching, silently daring me to cut to the chase.

I had the sense of sand slipping through my fingers no matter how tightly I clenched them. This was all going wrong, but then again, there was no way for it to go right. Considering her cold, hostile attitude, things weren't looking good. If Damian

Fields approached her now, promising money if it meant ruining me, she would've taken it without blinking.

I couldn't afford to take chances. It was time to backpedal and smooth things over. Yet, I had next to no experience with this outside of business. Personal issues were normally cut and dry. Then again, nothing about Rowan had ever been that simple.

After sipping my drink, I started again, cutting to the chase this time. "There is something important I need to discuss with you. But there's something else you need to know first."

The word contempt came to mind when she snorted. She'd had a lot of time to seethe over what I'd done. I couldn't blame her for that, but this attitude was starting to strain my patience. "I can hardly wait to hear whatever it is you think I need to know," she murmured, sipping her wine again.

I would walk away from this with bruised balls if she didn't let up a little. Nothing mattered more than keeping her on my side, keeping things civil if not friendly. Not that I would've minded a little warmth, especially since the proximity was beginning to stir up all kinds of memories, but I couldn't ask for too much. I'd settle for reaching an understanding.

"I looked for you. I didn't want to leave you

alone. You were transferred to another hospital, and nobody wanted to tell me where you went. I didn't know your real name. Besides…" I added, "Hospitals don't hand out personal information, not even when your last name is Collins. But I tried. I did."

She wasn't expecting that. For the first time since sitting, her haughty bitch attitude slipped. Her lashes fluttered, and for one brief moment, there was a sense of getting through the wall around her.

Until her jaw tightened, her teeth grinding almost audible as her gaze hardened to a glare. "Is that all you have to say? You didn't know my real name? Somebody certainly did."

If there was one thing I hated above all else, it was the sick sensation crawling its way up my spine as I fought to catch up with her meaning. Nothing irked me worse than being behind the curve. "What does that mean? Somebody? Who is somebody?" I asked.

She leaned in again, her voice turning to a hiss while a bright color bloomed on her cheeks. "Here's some news for you if you're really interested in catching up. I'm not the naïve little idiot I used to be. I'm not going to fall for a line about how hard you tried to find me after what happened. We both know that was never the real problem."

"I don't understand what you're talking about," I admitted. It was not something I felt comfortable announcing, but it was true. She had me at a loss. "What was the real problem?"

Again, her lashes fluttered before she shook herself a little. Her posture straightened, her chin lifted. "Why don't you tell me what your problem is instead? I have somewhere I need to be."

A date? The idea left me clenching my jaw. It was a strange reaction, considering how little I had thought of this woman in the years since I forced her out of my head. Since she vanished on me. Suddenly, she was in front of me again, and I couldn't imagine anything I'd like better than wrapping my hands around the neck of whoever she was in a hurry to see.

She arched an eyebrow, expectant, challenging me. "Anytime now," she murmured, which did nothing but take my blood from a simmer to a slow boil.

I had to remember what was at stake. I could handle a blow to my pride if it meant protecting what was mine. We had come too far for me to drop the ball now over a blonde with a wicked attitude. "Someone may approach you," I explained, watching her closely. "I need to know you aren't vulnerable to bribery."

"Excuse me? Bribery?" Her head snapped back, a look of confusion crossing her face. "Where is this coming from? What did you do?"

"It's all business." She leveled a disbelieving look at me, her mouth going thin in a smirk that threatened to get my blood boiling again. "It's true. An opponent has already used my business partner's past against him. Miles Young. You may have heard something about him in the media."

I was surprised when she shrugged. "Honestly, no. What line of work are you in? This is the first time hearing about you doing more than cruising around the strip, getting into trouble."

That, I couldn't believe. "You're lying."

Her face went slack for a second. "Excuse me?" she hissed. "You don't have the first idea—"

"Don't pretend you didn't google me the second you had a free minute today. Come on, Rowan." I sighed, shaking my head. For the first time since she sat down, I had the upper hand, and I wasn't about to squander it. "We're both adults. We both know how the world works. Drop the shit."

Folding her hands on the white tablecloth, she

offered an empty smile. "By all means." A wall may as well have come down between us. Hell, we may as well have been doing this over Zoom, hundreds of miles apart. That was how far she felt from me. It was easy enough to pretend it didn't strike me as sad, that I wasn't disappointed. The problem was, I couldn't lie to myself.

"I had hoped to approach this from a place of friendship," I made sure to tell her because I wasn't the one bringing hostility to the table. She needed to know that. "A piece of technology I'm looking to patent is being pursued by a competitor who plays dirty. He already scoured my partner's past and found something to dredge up. He's trying to stir up drama, get our investors questioning their involvement, all in hopes of slowing down our work so he can get the patent before we do."

I watched as understanding dawned. The slight softening of her gaze, the gentle parting of her lips once she realized what this was all about. "I see," she whispered. "You're afraid this will come out too." She waved a hand to indicate the thin web of scars that marred her otherwise perfect beauty.

"It occurred to me," I confirmed. "There's no delicate way to say it. Has anyone approached you?"

"That's all this was about? Making sure I keep my mouth shut?" She laughed softly while lifting the glass to her lips. Lips that used to feel so damn good sliding up and down my shaft. The thought hit me with surprising force, making me forget Damian and the patent and everything else but the increased pressure in my pants.

"You make it sound pretty ugly."

She touched a hand to her chest. "Oh, I'm so sorry to offend you. That's the last thing I would ever want to do." Finishing her wine, she almost slammed the glass onto the table. A couple sitting nearby noticed, giving each other a meaningful look before returning to their conversation.

Rowan either didn't see them or didn't care. Considering who I was dealing with, I would go with the latter. "Have you forgotten the contract I signed?" she asked.

There was more to the question than what was on the surface. I knew it, thanks to the intensity of her stare, almost like she was daring me to argue. The mention of a contract made my skin crawl. Did she think it was my idea to have it drawn up as if Dad would've given me a say in anything once I made the biggest mistake of my life? "I never saw the document, so I wouldn't know the terms," I explained, and it was the truth.

I had forgotten the sound of her laughter, the

way it started as a rumbling in her throat before bubbling up and out. It was almost bawdy, like a woman remembering a dirty joke she wanted to share. It never did match her almost supernatural beauty.

"Right," she barked out, her laughter dying as she abruptly dipped a hand into her bag and pulled out a wallet. "Well, this was fun. Thanks for catching up. You have nothing to worry about."

We were in public, meaning the impulse to restrain her had to be suppressed. My fists tightened under the table, trembling from the strain of staying civil for the sake of appearances. "Wait a minute," I gritted out through a tense smile, my eyes darting from side to side in case we had observers. The last thing I could afford was bad publicity. "Don't make this ugly."

"Me? You're accusing me of making things ugly?" There was that laughter again, and even as I stared at her in amazement, I couldn't help but remember hearing it late at night, in my bed, when we would talk until dawn. Wrapped up in each other, limbs tangled, sharing breath along with the rest of ourselves.

"Here's what's really happening, Spencer." She lifted a hand to signal for the server, holding up a credit card—the international symbol for *bring me the check now*. "You don't want your regrettable past coming back to haunt you and your business partner, whoever he is. That's what this is about, so let's not pretend otherwise. Don't worry," she concluded, looking at me with nothing but contempt. "I won't ruin anything for you. As usual, everything will go exactly the way you want it. Isn't that the way life has always worked for you?"

"Could we not turn this into something it doesn't need to be?"

"If anything, I should thank you for this little meeting. You showed me something I wasn't aware of until tonight. Four years of undergrad, three years of law school, busting my ass to pass the bar and survive my first associate position, and I'm still naïve as hell when it comes to you. I honestly thought for a second there that you might have invited me for a drink to clear the air. To apologize for what happened and how it happened."

"You hardly gave me the chance."

"Bullshit," she whispered. "If the roles were reversed, I would have dropped to my knees and begged forgiveness the second I saw you walk through the door. Nothing could've stopped me from making an ass out of myself in front of the whole world. But you have the nerve to sit there and act like I'm the reason you didn't get to apologize? Time hasn't changed you as much as you want me to think it has. You haven't changed a bit."

What was worse? The words she chose or the way they landed like the crack of a whip? It would've been easy to remind her she ran away, cut me off, couldn't be bothered to answer her phone the dozens of times I called, or leave a fucking forwarding address. Instead, I bit my tongue until the sting was too much.

It was enough to cut off what almost burst out of me and would, without a doubt, have left me with a dangerous enemy. "That's not true."

"It's not?" Her eyebrows damn near jumped off her forehead when they shot up all at once. "Then go ahead. Apologize. You've had more than ten years to come up with one, right? Let's hear it."

"Don't be a child," I scoffed. "I didn't come here to be put on the spot."

"Of course you didn't. You came here to cover your ass." She stood, shaking her head as she slung her bag over her arm. "Why would I consider paying the check? This is on you. Thanks for the drink."

No, no, she couldn't leave. Not like this. "Wait," I urged, standing.

"Don't bother." Pulling out her phone, she muttered, "Congratulations, your ass is covered. I signed a contract, and the terms were crystal clear. You have the nerve to sit there and act like you didn't know the first thing about it. You are so full of shit that I have to wonder if you even know how full of it you are."

"You are not leaving like this."

"Watch me," she whispered, tapping her screen. "My Uber is already on the way. It's been a real pleasure, Spencer." The venom dripping from her voice told another story.

I took a few steps behind her, intent on following when our server cut me off. "Your check, sir?" she asked, handing me a leather folder while Rowan stalked off without so much as a glance over her shoulder.

There was no choice but to let her go unless I wanted to start a scene. It pissed me off watching her leave, rooted to the spot when I wanted nothing more than to follow her. Catch her. Make her understand.

How was I supposed to convince myself she wouldn't tell the world I almost killed her when we were little more than kids? That I had crushed her dreams and walked away unscathed?

4

———

ROWAN

You idiot. What did you think was going to happen?

A bitter laugh leaked out of me as I covered my mouth with my hand. Tears dripped onto it, and now that I was alone in the back seat of a Ford Focus, I could let them flow. It would hardly be the first time I'd cried in the back of a car.

Damn him.

Damn me too.

What did I expect? For him to have this big moment where he cleared everything up? All my questions, confusion, and betrayal I wrestled with in those ugly early days. Lying alone in a hospital bed, seeing everything I had worked and hoped for falling to pieces.

The doctor's voice was soft, careful, but it felt like it was coming from underwater, muffled by the pounding in my ears. "The damage was extensive," he said, and each word seemed to sink deeper into my chest. but we're going to do everything we can to minimize the scarring." I swallowed hard, my throat suddenly dry, but the lump there wouldn't go away.

My fingers clenched the thin hospital blanket, knuckles going white as I tried to focus on anything but the word 'scarring.' His voice blurred into the hum of the machines beside me, but that one word echoed, bouncing around in my mind. Scarring. My stomach twisted painfully.

I blinked, eyes darting around the sterile room. This wasn't real. It couldn't be. "What am I doing here?" I croaked out, my voice barely recognizable. "Who's paying for all this?" Panic flared in my chest, my pulse quickening. I couldn't afford this. My family couldn't afford this. "I don't have a lot of money, and neither do my parents."

The doctor's hand landed gently on mine, his touch warm, but it didn't stop the cold creeping up my spine. "Don't you worry about that," he said, his smile kind but distant, like he knew something I didn't. "It's all been taken care of. All you need to concern yourself with now is recovering."

It was actually sad how long it took me to figure

things out. Obviously, Spencer was behind the transfer. He had paid for my surgeries without saying a word, without explaining himself, and definitely without an apology. Maybe to him, that was his apology. Maybe he expected me to be grateful for the money and not expect anything else.

I wiped away my lingering tears, clenching my jaw tight. Fuck this. I had cried more than enough. And I had made it through with no help from him but his money.

I couldn't pretend the money didn't help—it was the only reason I managed to build my career. What had felt so much like the end of the world at that time now looked a lot like a blessing more than a decade after the fact.

There were no blessings in sight when I was in that hospital bed, though. There was nothing but fear and dread and horror. *"Will you be able to fix me? All the way, I mean? Will you be able to make it so nothing shows?"* My heart ached now when I remembered whispering those words, tearful and desperate.

Another thing I appreciated about the doctor— he didn't bullshit me. *"We're going to do our best,"* he murmured, *but I heard the truth in his voice. "The damage was fairly extensive. A broken nose and cheek-*

bone, a partly severed ear, and a contusion to your scalp and temple. We'll need to wait for the worst of the swelling to go down before we can accurately assess and come up with a game plan for surgery."

I couldn't ask the real question that sat on my chest like a lead weight. He wouldn't have an answer, after all. He couldn't see into the future.

Will I ever work again? Will I be a star?

I released a deep breath, watching the world pass outside the window. I knew at the time. In my heart, I knew damn well. There wouldn't be any more acting, at least not the kind where I showed my face. There would be no more dreams of premiers, splashy magazine layouts, or fans screaming my name as I walked a red carpet. I wouldn't be Hollywood's next 'It Girl.' If anything, it would be a cautionary tale of why you don't get into a sports car with an irresponsible little shithead who never had to take life seriously or face the consequences of anything he's done.

He couldn't even apologize. That filthy, pathetic little coward. Was I under some level of delusion while we were together? I must have been. I couldn't think of another reason why I would fall for his shit.

At least, that's what I wanted to tell myself years later with the benefit of time and wisdom. It was easier to pretend I forgot what it was about him that made him irresistible, but that's all it was. Pretend.

I wasn't being fair to the girl I used to be, the one who passed up on a full scholarship in favor of trying to make it work in Hollywood. "Three years," I told Mom and Dad as a fresh-faced, hopelessly starstruck kid. "Just give me three years. If I can't make it work, I'll find a way to get through school without the scholarship. But I know I can do this. I know I can build a career out there."

I had been on my way to doing it too. It was so close I could almost taste it. Fame was just beyond my reach. Another part or two, a little more networking, and I would've had my big break. Or so I'd told myself for a long time after the accident.

That belief had festered in my soul, turning hard and bitter, eating a hole for me in the days immediately following the crash. When I first woke up to find nothing but excruciating pain gripping my head and face, I knew deep in my heart I was finished. That it was all over before it ever really began. That I would never see Spencer again.

I knew it even as that lawyer showed up with his damn contract and all his thinly-veiled threats about what would happen if I broke the agreement and reached out to the man who'd put me in the hospital. Who cared about promising never to contact him again when I already knew Spencer would never come back because what he had liked best about me was ruined?

Ruined by him.

It wasn't like I hadn't walked straight into my own destruction.

Well, I finally had closure. At least I could say that much for myself by the time the car exited the freeway and took the familiar route home. Funny how I couldn't think of it any other way, even if I hadn't lived here full-time in ages. This was the place that immediately came to mind when I thought of home. Not the apartment I'd been leasing for three years to be closer to the office and business-related events, but the little house in the valley where I had grown up and where everything that really mattered lived.

I felt stronger and more sure of myself as I climbed out of the car, thanking the driver. The only thing worth regretting about the evening was that I didn't get to watch Spencer's reaction as I left. Otherwise, I got the last word, and it was obvious he was thrown by my attitude. He deserved so much worse for throwing money at me and disappearing.

I made sure to leave my driver a generous tip,

then traveled the walkway, which Mom always kept neat and free of weeds that might otherwise choke the cheerful little flowers she tended within an inch of their lives. The lights were on inside the house, and I heard the television as I stepped up to the front door, using my key to unlock it.

"I'm home," I announced with a weary sigh as I walked into the living room. It would never make the cover of a decorating magazine, but the sight of over-stuffed furniture and framed photos clogging up the walls brought peace to my soul. Photos of me through the years—the star of the high school shows, local productions, even one of me on the set of my first commercial. No parents were ever prouder, even if the commercial was for antiper-spirants.

Something else caught my attention and held it. After eyeing the MacBook and texts lying open on the coffee table, I lifted my head at the sound of Mom's approach from the kitchen.

"What are you doing here?" she asked, confused but smiling. "We weren't expecting you tonight."

"I missed my girl." Again, I looked at the class-work on the table. "Are we studying in front of the TV now?"

"She was doing a group project on Zoom, and I

wanted her out here so I could listen in on the conversation while I cleaned the kitchen," she explained, drying her hands on a flowered dish towel. "I didn't recognize the car that dropped you off. Who was that?"

Eventually, my mother would have to get used to the idea of me being a grown woman. "An Uber," I replied. "I left the car at the office tonight. I wound up meeting someone for a drink and thought it would be safer not to drive."

That was as much as I would tell her. Not that she would recognize his name—I had never used it, not once. Even while we were dating, back when I entertained fantasies of a life in the spotlight and a future with Spencer, a playboy whose family money meant he lived in a completely different world. I had been so afraid of telling them about him. It all seemed so big and fraught with complications, and that was back before he ended my lifelong aspirations. The sort that left a parent paying for acting and dance lessons, not to mention forcing them to accept the idea that their little girl wasn't going to take the typical path through life. How many people got a full scholarship and turned it down in favor of chasing a dream?

Her furrowed brow smoothed, and then she chuckled lightly. "Of course. My responsible girl."

I wasn't always so responsible, was I? Now, I wished I had told her his name back then so I could now tell her how he had insulted me at the bar, treating me like some second-class citizen, a mouth he needed to shut so I didn't make things difficult for him. Poor baby. Was this the first difficulty he had ever come up against?

"Where is she?" I asked, sliding out of my stilettos with a grateful sigh. What a shame they made my legs look so good, considering they were torture devices.

"She went up to take a shower." Mom returned to the kitchen, whistling softly. The sound followed me up the stairs, where I passed two closed bedroom doors and knocked on the last one at the end of the hall—my childhood room. Light streamed out from under the door, along with a telltale sound that left me smirking as I knocked louder.

"Just a second!" The sound of the video game cut out, then I heard, "Come in."

I had to remind myself to fix my face as I slowly opened the door. Hannah was sitting cross-legged on the bed, her blonde hair hanging wet and loose around her face. She'd chosen one of my old school T-shirts to wear to bed, making her ten-year-old body look even smaller in comparison. There was a book open in her lap and everything. She was working hard to sell the lie that she'd been reading rather than playing a game.

"Hey, there," I murmured with a smile. "Did you have a good day?"

"Mom!" She got up on her knees, arms outstretched, and I wasted no time wrapping mine around her. My heart calmed now that I had her close to me. I buried my nose in her clean and sweet-smelling hair. When I closed my eyes, I almost remembered her delicious newborn scent. I lost track of the many hours I'd spent soaking in that glorious sweetness. If only I could have bottled it.

She was clinging to me a little tighter than usual, worrying me as I stroked her hair. "So, how did it go at school today?" I asked, kissing her forehead and sitting on the bed. She joined me, and I absently picked up the brush from her dresser and began working on her hair.

With a grunt, she announced, "Jason Gonzalez is such a dick."

"Language," I warned, fighting back a grin. It was still a challenge, hiding my amusement whenever she came out with something like that—exactly the sort of thing I would've said if I were dealing with a dick like Jason.

"Sorry. Jerk," she amended with another grunt. "He wouldn't stop making noises during my presentation in World History. He kept trying to distract me. I lost my place right in the middle of Archduke Ferdinand's assassination."

"Ouch," I murmured, gently brushing out a few tangles.

"But I got through it." The pride in her voice stirred pride in my chest. My fierce little girl.

"I know you did because that's who you are. You don't let anybody with a big mouth push you around." We had that in common. I had faced a bigmouth bully today.

"Aunt Ree was here for dinner but left before helping Grandmom with the dishes. She said she had something to do tonight."

"I'm glad she did, though I'm sorry I missed her. I'll have to give her a call." Rhiannon had only moved out for good a few years ago, around the time I leased my apartment. She said Hannah didn't need her anymore. I'd disagreed, but at the same time, she deserved a life of her own. I hated to think of her using my daughter as a reason for holding herself back.

"I think she works too much," my wise, all-seeing daughter decided. "Even more than you." I couldn't disagree, though Rhiannon certainly made enough money to compensate for the time she spent as part of a team of programmers.

"You don't miss anything, do you?" I asked, peppering kisses along her ear and cheek.

"I'm not some dumb kid," she reminded me. "I notice things. So what did you do tonight before you came over?"

She would have to go and ask me that, wouldn't she? Did she notice the way the question froze me for a second as I got hold of myself?

I was having a drink with your father. Nope. That would never happen. She would never know him, and not only because it would be too much of a shock after all these years growing up without a dad. It had taken ages to get to the point where she stopped asking about him. Eventually, she had gotten used to the idea of her grandfather being the closest thing to a dad she would have—unless I got married, which wasn't looking likely.

I was fine the way I was and didn't need anything else. I had my baby. I had parents who had taken so much on their shoulders to make sure I could make the best of what extended family members used to call *The Tragedy*—the tragedy of my accident and giving up on my dreams.

"Catching up with an old friend," I told her, which was as close to the truth as I dared to venture. Bringing him into our lives would mean leaving her open to the world he'd grown up in and still inhabited. A world where other people were nothing more than amusements, something to enjoy, use up, and discard when the good times were over, and where he could destroy my dreams and walk away from his responsibilities, including the little girl whose hair I finished brushing out. He hadn't asked about her or whether there was a child in the world with an impish smile so much like his. No doubt, he assumed I ended the pregnancy after the accident, and he deserted me. Let him call me selfish, but I didn't want him anywhere near her.

"Want me to braid your hair?" I asked. She deserved for me to be present with her, in the moment, not wallowing in past bitterness.

"Sure. It will be wavy in the morning." She handed me a hair tie from a little bowl on her dresser, and I got to work. What a relief she was still young enough that it was easy to distract her.

"Do you want to come back here tomorrow after school, or do you want me to send an Uber to school that will take you to the apartment?" One day, she would live with me full time. I could hardly wait until the day came. To feel like a real family, just the two of us. For now, it made more sense for her to stay here during the week to maintain a sense of continuity without requiring a long ride to and from school, not to mention my schedule, which was unpredictable, to say the least.

I couldn't guarantee I would be home for her when she needed me.

It meant having a deadline of sorts. By the time she left the eighth grade and was ready to start high school, I needed to have my shit together. I needed a stronger client list and a staff to handle things so I could take a step back and make myself available to my daughter.

For now, we were together on the weekends, back at my apartment, where I had set up a bedroom for her, which resembled the one here for the sake of familiarity. If anybody might replicate it, it was me since I had stared at the delicately flowered wallpaper and ruffled white curtains for years. One day, she would decorate it on her own when it was her full-time home.

"How late are you staying?" She let out a soft yawn that she tried like hell to cover up. My heart swelled, knowing she was only trying to cover up her sleepiness in hopes of spending more time together.

"I was thinking about staying the night, if that would be okay with you. If you wouldn't mind sharing the bed."

Her head snapped around, eyes sparkling. "Really? What about work tomorrow?"

"I don't have any meetings until ten o'clock, so that gives me plenty of time to go to the apartment and get dressed and everything. What do you think? Can we have a little sleepover tonight?"

"Sure." She hopped off the bed, rushing around to pull things from the dresser. "There's lots of stuff in here for you to wear. But oh, I didn't clean up my stuff downstairs yet."

"Why don't you go down and do that, then say good night to Grandmom and Grandpa while I get changed?" The question was barely out of my mouth, and she was scampering from the room. On the way down the stairs, she announced to Mom that I was spending the night.

Mom had asked why I came here tonight instead of going home like I normally would have. This was why. I had to be with my baby after seeing him. I had to take what was mine and cling to it, hold it close, and remind myself what really mattered. Spencer had taken so much away from me, but he had given me Hannah. When I was too tired to keep going, every time I wanted to give up and close the books and say to hell with it, all it ever took was the thought of my little girl.

I was lucky. There were no illusions, now or back then. As I got undressed and pulled on a soft, much-loved T-shirt and shorts, I offered a silent prayer of thanks to the universe for giving me parents who hadn't said *I told you so*, hadn't chastised me, or worse, for getting pregnant. Always, they wanted to know what they could do to help. What would make my life easier. It had meant moving home, living here during school, with the folks and Rhiannon taking care of Hannah when I couldn't.

I had it better than so many others could dream of, and I would not let Spencer take that away from me. I wouldn't let him take Hannah and turn her into the sort of spoiled, self-centered person he was. The fucker had never apologized, never took responsibility for crashing that car.

What a shame for him because it meant losing out on a hell of a kid. Somebody he might have been proud of. Somebody who had his eyes and a wicked intelligence she made sure nobody ever forgot about.

"All set!" Hannah announced as I finished washing my face in the bathroom sink. "Can we put on a movie? If we keep the volume down real low so it won't keep me up?"

"Only if you make me a promise." I finished drying my face, glancing at her in the mirror when she stood behind me. "From now on, no sneaking off to your room to play video games until you've cleaned up after yourself downstairs. Deal?"

"Deal," she mumbled, chewing her lip. "Sorry. I was waiting all day to play."

"I get it." I tugged her braid on the way down the hall, savoring her giggles. There would come a day when she wouldn't be so eager to spend time with me. I needed to take in as much of it as I could while I had the chance.

It took her no time to fall asleep, regardless of how excited she was to have a sleepover. She left me lying awake, staring at the television without following the movie she chose, remembering the man who'd helped create her and how thoroughly he had crushed my heart.

5

SPENCER

It was rare for me to wake up in my sun-drenched Beverly Hills bedroom.

Almost as soon as I came home from the overseas trip that Dad forced on me, I got a place in the Bay Area. Knowing what I wanted to do with my life meant the need to be close to the action. That meant moving to Silicon Valley.

I didn't have the heart to get rid of this place, though. It had come in handy. There were nights over the years when I'd crashed here after partying harder than expected. I've loaned it to friends, though that's something I stopped doing after a Fourth of July weekend that ended with a tearful call from my cleaning lady and more than a little redecorating. Sometimes, it didn't pay to be generous.

Saying Rowan was the first thing to go through my mind when I opened my eyes wouldn't be quite true since thoughts of her never stopped once I closed them. I had fallen asleep after hours of thinking about her. She was the star of every dream last night. The accident, of course—vivid and graphic and so damn real. Though, it wasn't the only thing. I closed my eyes again, trying to hold onto the memory of her at the club.

Then, the world around me faded, and I was back in the crowded, dimly lit club. The air was thick with the scent of beer, sticky liquor soaking into the worn floors. The thrum of bass pulsed through my chest, vibrating up my spine as voices rose and fell in an almost primal roar. Bodies pressed together, jostling for space at the bar, a hot, chaotic wave of people, but all I saw was her.

She was there, behind the counter, pouring drinks with a practiced grace that made it look easy. Her ponytail swung with every movement, catching the light just right, gleaming like gold. Her smile cut through the noise, wide and unguarded, as if nothing could touch her here, in this moment. I watched the way her eyes caught the room—bluer than the ocean, bluer than anything I'd ever seen. It's like she knew something the rest of us didn't.

How wasn't every man here hopelessly in love with

her? I couldn't tear my gaze away, and for a second, it felt like I was the only one who saw her for what she was— more than the usual faces that blended into the city nightlife. There was nothing typical about her. She moved like she owned the space, her steps light, quick, her presence magnetic.

It wasn't her beauty that had pulled me in like a fish with a hook in its mouth. It was her. The warmth she exuded. I could hardly hear a word she said, but I felt her genuine decency like a quiet warmth settling over me. She wasn't flirting, shoving her tits in my face in hopes of a bigger tip. There was nothing false about her.

I found out later that night the rest of her was very real too. My hands and mouth had examined every inch of her body until I had her memorized.

There was another regret to be added to the rest. I was a dumbass kid then, twenty-two, thinking I had the answers when it came to taking care of a woman's pleasure. What I had lacked in skill, I made up for in stamina. Now, with another decade-plus of experience under my belt, I could make her toes curl in record time.

The thought took my concentration and moved it south, thickening my dick. I couldn't stop the groan that vibrated in my throat. Fuck, she was a living sin, strikingly beautiful beyond words.

She responded to my touch with a palpable intensity —her eyes dilated, and her breath quickened, betraying the heat that surged through her.

She loved it like this, from behind, relishing the way I filled her as I gripped her hips and drove into her. Her squeals and desperate pleas for more sent a fire through me that I didn't want to be doused.

Memories of her were vivid. *Her fists twisted in the sheets, her ass jiggling. She loved it when I wrapped her hair around my fist and tugged.*

She had made me feel like a king, claiming her, fucking her until she was a pretty, sweaty mess.

I was hard as steel by the time I wrapped my fingers around my shaft. The precum oozing from my tip served as lube. I used it, coating my cock, imagining it was her tight, hot cunt clenching around instead. Or her mouth. She loved giving head and would get wet sucking on my length, bobbing up and down. Sometimes, I would have her turn around so I could eat her pussy, while other times, I'd settle for fingering her while she gave me great head. Those muffled, throaty moans used to drive me crazy.

The sound of my breathing filled the room as I

fucked my fist with her face in my mind's eye and the memory of her whispers in my ears. "*Fuck me, Spencer. Make me come for you.*"

My long, low groan was an exclamation point, filling the bedroom as I spurted once, twice, still indulging in memories that had been locked away for years, waiting to be brought out one day.

One thing was clear by the time I got out of bed and walked naked to the bathroom—I had to see her again. No way would I leave things as they were, with her walking out on me. I couldn't let the team down by risking the worst. There had to be a way to smooth things over.

My mind was made up by the time the first beads of icy water hit my skin. Cold showers always snapped me out of any lingering brain fog, which was what I needed after a restless night full of broken dreams.

There was another task I had to tackle first. My heart was heavy when, still wrapped in a towel post-shower, I texted Miles. He deserved to know what I was juggling, especially since he'd come clean with me the minute we heard Damian was digging into his past in London.

Me: *Give me a call when you can. Not an emergency.*

My phone rang not five seconds after the text

went through. "I told you it's not an emergency," I answered by way of greeting. "The last thing I need is a new bride on my ass for waking her husband up early on their honeymoon."

Miles yawned, then snorted with laughter. "It's not a problem. I'm jet-lagged to hell and back, anyway. What do you have for me?"

"I hate to do this to you on your honeymoon, but..." It was like ripping off a Band-Aid. Better to get it over with right away, all at once. "Honest to God, I hadn't thought about her in years," I concluded after giving him the condensed version of our history. "I wasn't trying to keep it from you."

He kept me waiting for what felt like an eternity before grunting. "I'm glad you told me about this. I take it no one else knows?"

"Not even my closest friends here in town. Only my father and his lawyer, and we never discussed it again." As far as Dad was concerned, it never happened. He sent me to China to work in our shipping offices and washed his hands of the whole thing.

"And the girl," Miles added.

"And her."

"What are you going to do about her? Do you think she's a threat?"

"Don't worry about that," I told him, gazing out the windows overlooking downtown. She was out there somewhere, going about her life the way she had all this time like I didn't exist.

It bothered me more than it should have.

"Respectfully, I'm a little worried." He sounded so damn British when he said it.

"We'll be fine. She kept mentioning the contract, and she's a lawyer. She knows better than to break a binding agreement." Because, of course, Dad wouldn't leave anything to chance. I'd been too fucked in the head at the time to think much about it —worried for Rowan, hating myself, guessing she hated me twice as much. I was unable to reach her, obsessed with finding her, always waiting for somebody to show up at the front door with a warrant for my arrest. It was only when he mentioned the agreement she'd signed that my fears cooled a little, but he'd immediately dropped the bomb about sending me to China to hedge our bets and keep my reputation intact. I was too relieved at the time to question it.

The whole thing made my head spin more than a decade later.

"Exactly what was in this contract?"

"To tell you the truth, I never saw it." When he

groaned, I continued, "If there's one person my old man always had faith in, it was his lawyer. Jarvis Daniels. The man could work miracles, though I don't think God or Heaven had much to do with it." Speaking his name brought his image to mind. I had never seen him out of a dark suit like he was always on his way to a funeral.

"I suppose a lawyer would know better than to break a binding contract." I couldn't tell whether Miles was coming around or trying to convince himself. It didn't matter either way. I knew what I was talking about, and that was enough for me.

"Go enjoy your honeymoon. I'll keep you posted." Setting the phone aside, I heaved a sigh. Dad and Jarvis had jumped through hoops to keep me from facing the consequences of that awful, reckless night.

After a frantic 911 call, I'd immediately called Dad, who'd ordered me to keep my mouth shut and wait for Jarvis to arrive. All it took was a horrific, completely avoidable crash and the unconscious, blood-covered girl beside me to turn an arrogant prick into a terrified little boy begging Daddy for help, imagining nothing but an empty life ahead of me, my name forever tainted.

It was hard to imagine how many people he paid

off to keep me out of the narrative, remove my car from reports, and have reports destroyed altogether. He'd systematically covered up the entire thing.

But then again, there was nothing money couldn't do. It had the power to make a person disappear the way I had disappeared, whether I liked it or not. At the time, thinking Rowan had to hate me and wished we had never met, leaving the country seemed to make sense. What else did I have to keep me in California?

I had taken the coward's way out, and there was now a chance of it coming back to haunt us unless I found a way to make sure Rowan wouldn't decide to retaliate.

"IS MISS MCNULTY AVAILABLE? I need to see her."

The cute redhead behind the reception desk frowned ever so slightly. "Are you the gentleman who called earlier this morning asking for an appointment?"

"I am," I told her, as if telling me Rowan was busy would make a damn bit of difference.

She sighed loud enough to get the point across. I was a pain in the ass she didn't have time for. "Like I told you on the phone, she is in the middle of a conference and rarely accepts walk-in appointments, Mr...."

"Collins. Spencer Collins." I lowered my voice, cocking an eyebrow while delivering a slow smile that never failed. "Trust me. She'll want to see me, and I won't take up too much of her time."

Her stony expression softened the way I knew it would. "I'll see what I can do." Still, she looked like she wished I had never walked through the door as she picked up her phone and dialed an extension. When it was clear I wasn't going to do the gentlemanly thing and walk away, she turned slightly away in her chair, mumbling.

Rowan would see me. Not because she wanted to but because curiosity wouldn't let her turn me down. She wouldn't want me to think of her as a coward, either. Time might have changed some things, but it couldn't change a person's nature. There was a reason we clicked the way we did back in the day, and it wasn't purely physical. Something in her had appealed to something in me.

Though the physical aspect was definitely there.

"I just want to be famous." Her voice was soft, wistful. She traced invisible shapes on my chest with one polished fingernail, sighing. "I want to stand up there on

a stage while holding an award. I want to soak in all the applause. I want those blinding lights in my eyes."

I shouldn't have chuckled. Her head snapped up, eyes flashing. "What? You don't think I can?"

"Relax." I folded an arm under my head, laughing when she swatted my hand away from her shoulder. "Why do you always get pissed off before I get a chance to explain?"

Her body sagged against mine a little as she whispered, "I guess you don't know what it's like when all you ever hear is people laughing at your dreams."

"Mr. Collins?" I turned around to face the receptionist and her strained smile. "Miss McNulty finished the conference early so she could accommodate you." *It had better be worth it.* She didn't have to say it out loud. I got the message.

Rather than remind her I'd told her so, I followed her through the small office. It was almost quaint, not much more than a well-decorated hole in the wall. I would have to keep my opinions to myself —something told me Rowan wouldn't appreciate hearing them.

What was I doing? Flying blind by the seat of my pants. Last night left a bad taste in my mouth. She could fall back on that contract all she wanted, but I needed to be sure.

And dammit, she'd had the last word. That didn't sit well with me, either.

She sat behind a modern, sleek desk in a similarly appointed office with a decent view of downtown. Her sleeveless, sky-blue dress almost matched her eyes and showed off her firm body without revealing too much. Sexy as all fuck.

"Can I get you something to drink?" the receptionist asked me while Rowan stared at her computer screen, fingers tapping the keys.

"No, thank you." What I needed was for her to leave us alone. She did that soon enough, closing the door behind her, leaving me standing in the middle of the room like a jackass.

"I said everything I had to say last night." Rowan was still typing, focused on the screen, effectively ignoring me. "Everything is settled, and you have nothing to worry about. But thank you for giving me an excuse to get off the phone. I was bored out of my mind."

"Don't tell me that's all you care about."

"Getting off the phone?" she asked.

So this was the game she wanted to play. "Everything being settled," I gritted out.

Her head snapped around almost eerily fast. "What if it is?" She was glaring, but she was looking at me. At least, she could give me that much courtesy.

"Do we have to leave things like this?" If there was ever a time for my charm to come to the rescue, it was now. I flashed a grin, approaching the desk with my hands in my pockets. "You mean to say after all these years, there's nothing but hostility? I've already explained that I wanted to be there for you."

"And I appreciate that. I understand now." Her fingers drummed faintly on the desk, something I pointedly ignored.

Taking a seat without waiting for permission, I shrugged. "Why don't we try again?"

She gave a start like an electric current ran through her, asking, "Try what, exactly? Because I think we're past the dating stage. And thanks to you, I'm now allergic to irresponsible playboys."

"Then it's a good thing I'm no longer irresponsible," I reminded her with a smirk while devouring her with my gaze. She had no idea what that icy attitude did to me, how it made me want to melt her down.

"Meaning what?" she asked, suspicious.

Meaning you look like mortal sin in that dress, and I want an excuse to peel it off you. "Meaning, let me take you for dinner tonight. Believe it or not, I would like to know more about your life."

Her teeth sank into her lip, and fuck me. Everything the woman did was designed to drive me crazy. I had the feeling the last thing she hoped for was my hands anywhere near her body, meaning she wouldn't intentionally turn me on.

Down, boy. Here I was, concerned with a possible scandal over the crash, and now I was looking at the possibility of a harassment suit if I popped a boner out of nowhere.

With her eyes downcast, she murmured, "There isn't much to know."

Did she know what a bad liar she was? "Tell me something. In your particular type of law, do you have to do a lot of bluffing? If you do, you might want to get better at it."

"That's enough. You can go now. Honestly," she insisted, shooing me toward the door with one hand. "You can go your way with a clear conscience. I made it through. I came out on the other side, and I'm doing better than ever. I don't need you to take me to dinner to smooth things over, and I'm not particularly interested in what life looks like for you nowadays."

"Are you sure about that?" Because, again, she

wouldn't look me in the eye. Not for long, averting her gaze like it hurt to look at me. Like she was lying.

"Sorry to inform you." Her full lips curved in a sarcastic, sugary smile. "But you are not that fascinating."

"I think you're lying."

"And I think you're unbelievably full of yourself," she retorted.

"Oh, I know I am." The line hit home, and her small giggle told me I was winning the battle. "You don't even want to know how I ended up getting into tech?"

For the first time since we met up yesterday, her mouth switched to something dangerously close to a genuine smile. "Probably because it's the opposite of what your father would want you to do? Just taking a shot in the dark."

I'd wondered if she would remember. That slight touch of familiarity boosted my confidence. "Something close to that. But I won't elaborate now. It's the kind of story that should be shared over dinner."

She ran a hand through her hair, then tucked it behind her ear. The strangest urge took hold of me while I watched. I wanted to be the one doing that— touching her soft hair and even softer skin. It had been a long time. With memories flying hard and fast, I was a starving man craving sustenance in the form of her body.

Her shoulders sank as she informed me, "I already have plans tonight."

So much for the semi beginning to stir in my pants. "You said that last night."

"It was true last night, too," she snapped. "What, you think I've waited around all these years for you? I have a life."

Undeterred, I suggested, "Tomorrow, then. Or Sunday, or any night. I would make time for you."

"Well, maybe that's because you're scared I'll ruin your—" Her eyes closed before a sigh slipped out from between her parted lips. "That was wrong. I shouldn't have said that."

"It's fine." It wasn't, but I had a business to protect. People were counting on me.

In a softer voice, almost defeated, she asked, "Can I let you know? I'll call you." When I smirked, she groaned. "I will. I have to check on a few things first, that's all."

"You're a busy woman," I observed, feeling better now that I'd won this round.

"I am." Clearing her throat, she sat up straighter in front of a wall covered in diplomas and certificates. She was proud of herself. She deserved it.

"Now, if you'll excuse me, I have something else I need to do. Don't you have an office to get to?"

That was the thing. What I was doing in her office was business. Just not the way she thought of it. "My office is wherever I want to be. I'll be waiting to hear from you."

I had planned on spending time in my office today, but there was nothing that couldn't be moved. Not that I couldn't take the jet back here at the last minute, but I didn't feel like going through the hassle if she decided to cancel her plans for the night.

"Is that your idea of a good closing line?" she asked as I strolled from the room.

For the sake of making sure she didn't change her mind, I kept my mouth shut, offering the receptionist a parting grin and taking the elevator down to the ground floor.

Walking down Wilshire Boulevard, I considered asking Lex to meet for drinks later. That was until Rowan's text came through. It had barely been five minutes since I left. She wasn't as standoffish as she wanted to pretend.

Rowan: *Tomorrow night. Don't make me regret this.*

There was no hope of fighting off a grin that caught the eye of a passing goddess who smiled back invitingly. On another day, I might have taken her up on that silent invitation. Not when the pleasure of knowing I got under Rowan's skin was so much more enjoyable. If anything, her hostility heightened the challenge.

This wasn't about placating her, not anymore.

There was no ring on her finger. Fair game, as far as I was concerned.

By the time our night together was over, she would remember everything that made us so good together in the first place.

6

ROWAN

It's dinner. Just dinner. Get a grip on yourself.

The mascara wand trembled as I touched it to my lashes, meaning I needed to take a breath and steady myself or end up looking like a fucking raccoon.

Hannah, thankfully, was unaware of how her mother was falling apart. "You look gorgeous, Mom." My daughter gave me a sage nod, walking around me in a slow circle, then letting me lean in close to the mirror in my apartment's generously sized bathroom. She even had the nerve to tap a finger against her chin while pursing her lips thoughtfully. "Ten out of ten, no notes."

Since when did she talk like a jaded reality show star? "You need to stop watching so much junk TV."

However, I did appreciate the compliment while pawing through makeup strewn across the marble vanity. If I didn't calm down, I'd start sweating like a pig. Very unsexy.

"She doesn't get that from TV." My sister leaned into the room, giving Hannah a playful scowl. Lucky for me, she was able to babysit. "That's the kind of stuff she and her friends say to each other all the time."

There was nothing judgmental about the way she said it. I didn't get the feeling that there was anything behind her words but the love of an aunt for her niece. Somebody who would drop everything to babysit on a Saturday night so her sister could make the questionable decision to go to dinner with the wrong man. Putting it mildly.

But dammit, that didn't stop me from going stiff before I caught myself and let it go. "I can't keep up with everything these kids say nowadays. And hearing myself say that, I feel old."

"You don't look old," Hannah offered, closing the lid on the toilet seat and plopping down to watch me put on my makeup.

"You are my favorite daughter," I told her, winking in the mirror.

"I'm your only daughter."

"That was sort of the point." I glanced toward my sister, and we shared a grin. We hadn't always gotten along very well—not that we were at each other's throats, but there was a phase where Rhiannon couldn't stop comparing us. If I got something for my birthday, she wanted it for hers, that sort of thing. We needed an equal number of Christmas presents under the tree, the same number of people invited to birthday parties, the same model of bike.

It was an obsession with her for a long time until she finally grew out of it in high school. That was when she started coming into her own as a student, winning computer science fairs and making friends at tech camp. I was glad for her, especially since it gave her something to be interested in. Now, she was a kickass programmer.

It gave her something to feel proud of too. I always felt bad for the way Mom and Dad highlighted my victories much more than hers. I had asked them to lay off more than once, but they had gently laughed it off. Sometimes, it was possible to love somebody so much that it could cloud judgment.

Hell, I knew that one from firsthand experience.

"So, who is the lucky guy deserving all this makeup and jewelry and everything?" Rhiannon asked, sizing me up while twirling a strand of hair a shade darker than mine around her finger.

"Nobody important. Really," I added when she rolled her eyes. "It's not a big deal."

"I don't know. What do you think, kid?" I caught her winking at Hannah in the mirror.

"It looks like you're going out with somebody you like." Hannah covered her mouth with her hand, eyes bulging. "Do you have a boyfriend?"

"No, I don't, and that's the truth. You don't have to be boyfriend-girlfriend with somebody to go out for dinner. It's just somebody I used to know."

"Somebody you used to know who is a boy?" she asked with more giggles.

"Maybe you're the one who should go to law school," I concluded with a groan that made my sister laugh.

"Come on, kid." Rhiannon held out a hand. "Let's go make some popcorn and find a movie to watch. Mom doesn't feel like being honest with us."

"Don't make it about that!" I called out after them, not that it mattered. They were busy giggling together, acting like the best friends they were.

It made me happy to see them get along the way they did, like peanut butter and jelly, an unbeatable duo. I had nothing to complain about when it came to my relationship with Hannah. We were close. She loved me, looked up to me. There wasn't any resentment, at least none that I noticed. She didn't hold it against me that I spent so much of my time away from her.

Still, part of me mourned the time I had lost with her. I was in class the morning she took her first steps. Every day, I would come home to a new milestone, which my parents had enjoyed. It meant I was a bystander in my daughter's life. All I could ever do was hope she would understand one day.

What some people might have called selfishness was a sacrifice almost too painful to describe.

I wasn't getting anywhere by standing around, getting emotional. Spencer's momentary return to my life had knocked me on my ass and left me thumbing through memories, both good and otherwise. Narrowing my eyes at my reflection, I lifted my chin in defiance.

It was dangerous to let myself indulge in the past. If I wasn't careful, I might end up wishing for all the things my heart had longed for during those lonely times when I wondered what would happen when Hannah asked about her father one day. I used to dream about him, imagining him coming back into our lives. As much as I resented him for running away after the crash, I wanted him more, not only for her but for me.

Those days had passed, and any feelings I had for him went hard and cold until they weren't anything more than the scars I now barely noticed. They had been part of me for so long, there were times I could forget about them, at least until I got one of those inevitable looks from a stranger. Some-times full of pity, sometimes curiosity.

What did that girl do to herself?

I would've told them if they had the nerve to ask. It was simple. I made the mistake of falling in love with the wrong person, someone who didn't have the balls to stay by my side after taking everything I ever wanted and crushing it under the wheels of his Lamborghini.

One thing was for sure. He would remember how good I looked tonight. I'd pulled out all the stops, from a trip to the salon with Hannah to an afternoon shopping trip where I picked up a new dress that looked like it was made for me. Sleek and black, the satin flowed like inky water over my breasts, down to my hips, and over the curve of my backside. I checked the knee-length hem, turning around to look at my back in the mirror. It was cut too low for me to wear a bra, baring more skin than I was comfortable with.

I felt sexy. When was the last time I let myself feel that way? Normally, I tried to tone down my looks a little, determined to be taken seriously. Now, I might as well have been Cinderella stepping into her pumpkin carriage as I strode down the hall of my corner apartment, heels clicking while the sound of laughter led me past the kitchen and into the living room.

Rhiannon and Hannah were on the sofa with a big bowl of popcorn between them. Hannah gasped when she saw the finished product of all of my preparation. "Mom. I want to date you."

Her sudden announcement made me burst out laughing, and my sister joined me. "So you like everything? The earrings are okay?" I touched my fingertips to the dangling diamond earrings I bought after signing my first client. I loved how they sparkled with every move I made, but I was starting to wonder if they were maybe a little too much.

I didn't want Spencer to think I went overboard for him, even if I had. It had been forever since I went this far for a simple dinner. It was probably a waste of time, something I would regret once he inevitably said something painfully ignorant or completely stupid.

I wanted him to see what he was missing. If I couldn't show him our daughter for obvious reasons, I would have to show myself off a little. Looking at her now, I knew he was missing out. Was she? Was I holding her back by hiding her from him? I was only trying to protect her from ending up like him. Would she understand one day?

"Perfect," Rhiannon announced, giving me a thumbs-up. "He won't know what to do with himself, whoever he is."

"Your boyfriend," Hannah teased in a singsong voice.

"I'm telling you, he's not. Sorry to disappoint you." We were supposed to meet at eight, and a glance at my phone told me the time was quickly approaching. I couldn't stall any longer.

Why was I so freaked out?

Rhiannon popped up from the couch with a few last-minute questions, following me to the door while I looked through my clutch to be sure I wasn't forgetting anything. "It's a Saturday night, and she's hanging out with you," I concluded. "We can push bedtime to ten so long as you promise not to let her eat that entire bowl of popcorn beforehand."

"Yes, ma'am," my sister replied with a salute. "I'll let her eat a whole package of Oreos instead."

"You're hilarious."

"You're nervous," she retorted, laughing gently. "Fess up. Who is this guy? Why are you so freaked out?"

"I'm not freaked out."

"Right. That's why you've put more energy into getting ready for tonight than I've seen you put into anything for... I can't even remember."

"And maybe that's a problem. But you know how it is. She's more important," I whispered, glancing at my oblivious daughter, who sat glued to her movie, mindlessly eating popcorn without looking into the bowl. If anything, it was a nice change from the tablet Mom and Dad had insisted on getting her for Christmas, even though I'd asked them not to.

"Hey, that's what we're here for," Rhiannon reminded me. "It takes a village and all that, right?"

"Thank you." I kissed her cheek, then rubbed a smudge of red lipstick off her skin. Cherries in the Snow, the same shade worn by generations of women on Mom's side. We all shared the same fair complexion.

"So..." Rhiannon stopped me before I could

leave, lifting an eyebrow. "Last question is, when can I expect you home? Or should I?"

"I'll come home," I promised. "I'm telling you, it's not that kind of night."

"Right. Just do me a favor and keep me updated if anything changes."

"You are impossible." I called out my goodbyes to Hannah one more time then ducked out, down to the elevator. My ride would be waiting downstairs any minute, and something told me I would need more than a drink or two if I wanted to get through this meal. Better to have someone do the driving for me.

This was crazy. If I ended up hurt, angry, or wanting to kill Spencer at any point, it would be nobody's fault but my own. Why did I let him do this to me? What did it matter if he saw for himself what he had missed out on by taking the cowardly way out? It didn't change anything. He had still chickened out and sent Daddy's lawyer to do what he should have done himself.

He hadn't known my real last name? Somebody sure as hell had because my true name was on that damn document.

No, he hadn't tried hard enough to find me, was all. And now, afraid of what retaliation might look like for him, he wanted to smooth things over. Show me a good time, maybe get me a little drunk, make me remember the way things used to be.

Like I could forget.

Like a week had gone by without me thinking of him at least once as I looked at the baby we created, remembering those days together when anything had seemed possible. Then, the nights I had spent sitting up with Hannah, rocking her to sleep, wondering what life would be like if her daddy was still in the picture. There had been plenty of time to remember and regret.

I had to deliberately push all that off to the side, climbing out of the car in front of the West Hollywood restaurant. No doubt he chose some-place trendy and upscale to impress me. I wasn't the same girl anymore, the one who practically creamed her panties over an exclusive dinner reser-vation or a flight to San Francisco on his family's private jet.

That didn't mean I was immune to the reaction. He was waiting for me, standing in front of the building, distracted by something on his phone. I had the chance to observe him without him knowing it. Did that soft grunt come from me? It must have because it paired so well with the sudden ache in my chest and the consuming heat in my core.

All of a sudden, I was hungry. Starving. And food had nothing to do with it. He was so damn handsome, unfairly so, with his slightly mussed blond hair looking like he had just run his hand through it, pushing it back from his tanned forehead. His sharp jaw was perfectly highlighted by the light from his phone, and the firm set of his full mouth told me he was deep in thought. Oh, that mouth of his. The things it used to do to me.

The things I could almost imagine it doing to me now, caught up in the grip of blind lust that only got worse when his gaze lifted.

It wasn't an act—the breath he released, the way his shoulders sank, and his face went slack in those first seconds after he recognized me. He pulled himself together quickly, but not fast enough. All of my work had been worth it. A shiver of pleasure ran down my spine as I started walking toward him.

"You look incredible," he said as I approached, though he didn't need to. The rasp in his voice got the message across as his throat worked when he swallowed hard.

Oh God, was I in trouble. Because when was the last time a man had looked at me the way he was?

Not that I had gone celibate, but life had sort of gotten in the way. Beyond a couple of casual flings in law school, there hadn't been time or emotional bandwidth available for a relationship. And there had never been an opportunity to dress up like this outside of an industry event, where everybody jumped through hoops to outdo everybody else, and I faded into the background.

Not in years had a man stared at me with blank desire written across his face.

Not in years had there been a man I wanted to look at me that way.

I had walked into this dinner, telling myself it would be a miracle if I didn't kill him. Now, I was starting to think it would be a miracle if I ended the night with all my clothes on and my self-respect intact.

How was I supposed to fight him when I was too busy reminding myself to breathe whenever our eyes met?

"Shall we?" he asked, holding out his crooked arm to escort me inside. That effortless charm. It was more potent than ever, strong enough that I took his arm and told myself to let everything else go for tonight.

Just for tonight.

SPENCER

"It's been great. I feel like I've found my niche, you know?" What was left of our meals sat in front of us, cold by now. I had lost interest in my grilled salmon long before then. Not that it wasn't good.

The conversation was better. *She* was better. It took nothing more than two glasses of wine and a little food to loosen her up. Now, there was no holding her back.

And I couldn't pretend I wasn't interested. When had I had a conversation with a woman for the sake of conversation? Somewhere over the past two hours, my intentions had shifted. Right now, this had nothing to do with getting on her good side or covering my ass. "Making sure girls like you don't get taken advantage of by predatory studio executives?" I asked, noting her smirk.

"Yes, now that you put it that way. I know what to look for. And I know what it's like to be so young and hungry for success that you'd be willing to look the other way in certain situations." A cloud passed over her face like she was remembering something ugly, and the idea stirred anger in my chest. Had she been taken advantage of back then?

"What about you?" She finished the second glass of wine, setting it aside and leaning her elbows on the table, eyes sparkling playfully. It seemed like she was unaware of the attention she drew from men as they passed our table. I was aware of the way one animal recognizes the other out in the wild. *Back the fuck off*, I silently warned one such douchebag as he practically undressed her with his eyes. *She's mine tonight.*

"What about me?" I asked once my attention swung back to her and that glowing, tempting skin of hers. How much longer would I be able to keep my hands to myself?

"You said you would tell me how you ended up in tech." Her glossy lips stretched in a smile, drawing my gaze and waking my hunger. "I've been looking forward to hearing about it."

"Sorry to tell you, but I don't think the payoff will be worth the anticipation." When that didn't seem to make a difference, I chuckled. "I was working in China. Dad sent me there to '*turn me into a real person...*' his words," I added with a humorless snort.

"Nice," she muttered, shaking her head with a frown.

"Come on. We both know he had a point. He wanted me to learn more about the shipping business so I could step into his shoes when the time came. His plan backfired when I discovered logistics and how to streamline our processes. I started screwing around behind the scenes, digging into our data, learning how we harvested it and applied it to our growth. I even started looking forward to going to work."

"Wow. That's what you call finding what you're meant to do. I'm glad for you," she offered with a soft smile.

"It looks like we both found the path they were supposed to be on," I observed. It would be best to keep the rest of it to myself. She didn't need to hear about the crash being the catalyst since Dad sent me to China within a week after it. I wouldn't insult her that way.

One thing was for sure by the time we gave up on

eating and allowed the server to clear the table—the woman sitting across from me was miles away from the one who had barely stopped short of throwing her drink in my face two nights ago. She needed to get over the initial shock, to process what she was feeling. Come to think of it, so had I.

However, now that I had, the lines between what I needed to do and what I wanted to do were getting blurrier every minute. I'd told myself tonight would be about reminding her of the good times. What made us good together. The thing was, I was starting to remember that for myself.

And I wanted more.

Not for the patent. Not for my employees. Only for me. "I have an idea." Finishing my drink, I set the glass on the table and offered a challenging stare. "Why don't we enjoy a nightcap somewhere quieter, where we can continue this conversation?"

Her smirk showed up right on schedule. "Come on. You must have a smoother line than that."

"To tell you the truth, I don't normally need to use a line." When she rolled her eyes, I shrugged. "I haven't had much practice."

"Tonight was about dinner, remember?" What was it in her tone that told me she didn't mind? That knowing, teasing sound, so unlike a sharp rebuke. She had expected this.

"Dinner has been over for an hour, in case you didn't notice." I looked down at our plates, and she did the same. "I'm much more interested in you. If it would make you feel better, we can have a conversation in some packed, airless club. I wonder how long we would last before our voices gave out from all the screaming." She hesitated, giving me no choice but to break out the big guns. "I will bug the shit out of you every single day. You know I'll do it. I'm not going to let up until I'm satisfied."

"Exactly when will you be satisfied?"

A slow smile stretched my lips. "I couldn't tell you. It hasn't happened yet."

I had her. I knew it the second she grinned. "One drink at your place. I'll set a timer on my phone."

"You know how to make a man feel appreciated." She laughed off my sarcasm, waiting for me to settle the check while she pulled out her phone. "Don't tell me you're doing it now," I groaned, nodding to the device.

"No, for fuck's sake." She was chuckling as her thumbs tapped the screen. "Texting my sister, if you must know."

The Rowan I used to know would have almost swooned at the sight of the Bentley waiting for us at the curb once we left the restaurant. "Wow. They brought the car without you having to request it." That was what impressed her. Not the vehicle. She was a sophisticated woman now, not a wide-eyed girl.

"It's the little touches. This place is owned by a good friend of mine," I explained. "He's always talking about ways to set his businesses apart from the rest."

"Very smart." She wore a playful grin as she took my hand, allowing me to help her into the car. "Look at you, having smart friends. Times have changed."

She was right, which was why I couldn't do anything but laugh, closing the door. It wasn't long before we were on our way, the apartment only minutes from the restaurant, even on a Saturday night when traffic was dense. It occurred to me I wouldn't have minded getting stuck with her. It would mean an excuse to spend more time together.

There was something about her that was magic. I didn't have to pretend, didn't have to show off. I could be myself. How rare was that?

It was only when I pulled into the building's attached garage that she realized where we were.

"Wait a second. You still live here? In the same building?"

"Same building. Same penthouse."

"Get out! I guess some things don't change." She was laughing softly by the time we parked and headed into the lobby, shaking her head as she looked around at what hadn't changed much over the years. "My God. I feel like a time traveler. This is too funny."

"I remember you always loved the view," I reminded her, prompting her to smile up at me as the elevator carried us to the top floor. That smile. I had yet to meet another woman who radiated that tempting touch of wickedness. It was alluring, like so much about her. Heat raced through me and made my hands tremble with the need to touch her.

What a time for the elevator doors to slide open onto a quiet hallway directly across from my front door. Once I entered the passcode on the keypad, I swung it open and stepped aside, allowing her to enter first.

"You're kidding." She barely stifled a squeal, her heels clicking on the hardwood as she entered the living room. Tossing her purse on the couch, she turned in a slow circle.

"Like it?" I asked.

"This is such a trip." She laced her fingers on top of her head and blew out a heavy sigh that puffed her cheeks and pursed her lips. "It's just like I remembered it."

Which meant she had been thinking about it. I knew it. Running into each other had stirred up just as many memories for her as it had for me.

"I can't believe you kept the place." There was wonder in her eyes once she stopped gawking long enough to look my way. "All this time? You haven't been living here in Beverly Hills, have you?"

"No, the townhouse in San Francisco is home base. Close to the office. But with my family living nearby and friends out here, it made sense to keep the place."

She shot me a snide look on her way to the window. "A penthouse in Beverly Hills and a townhouse in San Fran. No need to brag."

"I don't have a need to brag. You know that." Motioning toward the bar opposite the sofa, I asked, "Drink? I have a nice Pinot Grigio you'd like."

Her brow furrowed long enough to tell me she was arguing with herself, but it was a short-lived argument. "Sure. But only one glass," she added, holding up a finger.

"Don't worry," I assured her as I rounded the bar

and reached underneath into the wine refrigerator. "I'm not trying to get you drunk and have my way with you. Though I'm not against the idea, either."

When she didn't snap at me, a warm sensation that felt a lot like victory swelled in my chest. She was loosening up, letting her guard down. That dress was as good as puddled on my bedroom floor. I would have to ask her to keep the shoes on. I practically felt the heels digging into my ass cheeks as I poured the crisp wine into a glass.

"I forgot how beautiful the view is from here." She was staring out the window, her back to me as I approached with her drink. The glow from so many lights below highlighted her hourglass figure to perfection. The woman was temptation itself, and no matter how I reminded myself not to push her too hard, there was only so long I could deny the natural need to reach out and stroke her arm.

Instead, I settled for touching her shoulder while I handed her the wine. It was electric. There was no other word for it, no way to explain it. It was undeniable, either way, the tremor that ran through me and demanded I take her in my arms. It was natural, as necessary as breathing. I had to hold her again. For closure, if for no other reason.

At least, that was what I told myself.

"Thank you." Her fingers stroked mine as she took hold of the glass, and I knew. She was in this with me. She wanted this as much as I did. If she didn't, she wouldn't have come here, wouldn't be looking at me the way she was, staring up at me with those big, shining eyes that held more truth than I'd ever seen anywhere else.

The air between us crackled when she turned to face me, swaying a little, leaning in. I lowered my head far enough to inhale the perfume in her hair, something sweet and floral with a hint of musk running underneath it. I needed that scent on my skin, on my pillows, all around me.

"What are we doing?" she asked, her voice faint.

"You tell me." My mouth grazed the top of her head while the backs of my fingers ran up and down her bare arms, enticing her, making her shiver.

"This shouldn't happen." Her whisper was weak, though, and she didn't lean away. No, she tipped her head back, hot breath fanning across my throat and making me shiver as her blue eyes met mine again.

I didn't answer in words. I settled for taking the glass back and setting it on a table near the window before taking her face in my hands, soaking in the field of her silky skin. I did not go into this evening expecting this. I couldn't have imagined wanting her this way. Not only her body but the undeniable rightness of being together. Had it always felt like this? Was I mature enough to understand it?

"Spencer..." Her eyes drifted shut, and a soft sigh eased its way from between her crimson lips. I had to taste them. I would die if I didn't.

She held her breath, and so did I in that last electric moment until I closed the gap between past and present by claiming her mouth again. I only thought I remembered the thrill of those plump lips against mine, the triumph of making her melt against me. I savored her, explored her, in no hurry to bring this to an end. We had all night, and I planned on using every last minute.

Her hands slid up over my chest, leaving fire in their wake. They moved over my shoulders, up to the back of my head. My nerves sang and sizzled when her fingers ran through my hair and over my neck, her touch passionate and tender. By the time her lips parted and her tongue stroked mine, I was rigid, my cock demanding satisfaction.

I backed her against the window, pinning her with my body, her tits heaving against my chest as I took her wrists in my hands and lifted her arms, holding them over her head. She moaned softly into my mouth and arched her back, grazing my bottom lip with her teeth and rolling her hips to tease my obvious, raging erection. Considering the way she shuddered, it seemed more like she was teasing both of us, reminding herself of what was waiting.

I broke the kiss, and she gasped, head falling back against the glass while my mouth moved down the slim column of her neck. Her pulse fluttered under my tongue, and she moaned helplessly, the throaty sound bringing back a flood of memories that left me growling and panting.

I had to let go of her wrists when there was so much more to touch. My hands slid down her arms, then her sides, finally landing on her hips, allowing me to pull her closer to where I ached for her. Her knowing groan was the sweetest torment.

I needed to be inside this woman.

How had I gone so long without her?

Her back arched again, tits heaving, begging for attention which I gladly gave with my mouth while inching the end of her dress higher, bunching it around her waist. When she parted her thighs in a silent invitation, I almost exploded then and there.

"Touch me," she begged in a desperate whisper while her heel ran up my thigh as she lifted her leg higher. She tilted her hips, determined to feel me against her. I wasted no time taking hold of her bare thigh, running my hand over her silkiness and stroking the curve of her ass, making us both gasp for air.

"You're so fucking sexy," I rasped against her tits, playing with her ass, making her squirm and writhe. Her breath came in short, ragged gasps that got louder when I found the center of her wet heat, probing her plump slit, my fingers gliding through her slick folds.

"Oh God," she whispered, moving against me, demanding her pleasure. I barely breathed, hardly thought. I was helpless, consumed with feeling her, wanting while working her into a frenzy. "Yes... yes!"

Of all times for her fucking phone to ring on the other side of the room. I ignored it, driving two digits deep inside her, searching for her G-spot, determined to make her come before sinking my cock inside her.

"Wait... no, wait, please." Her hands slapped my shoulders as she lifted me away from her half-covered chest with a groan. "I'm sorry, but that's my sister's ring. I need to take this."

Fucking hell. My fingers slid from her, and she lowered her leg, adjusting her dress as she darted across the room. All I could do was lean against the window, breathless and frustrated, suspecting an opportunity had passed me by. Not if I had anything to say about it. I would not be refused, not with her juices coating my fingers and my cock ready to burst from behind my zipper.

"Hello? Everything okay?" Almost immediately, she gasped. "Are you sure? What happened? Tell me everything."

One thing was for sure. She wasn't faking for the sake of getting out of the situation. There was genuine strain in her voice when I turned around to find her standing stock-still in the middle of the room, eyes bulging. She was looking my way, but she didn't see me. Not with that horrified look on her face. "He used my name? Did you see where he was from? I see. I'm on my way," she barked out. "No, don't do that. Just stay where you are, and I'll come to you. If it happens again, call the police right away. I'll be there as soon as I can."

She was shaking as she ended the call, her hand falling to her side. "What happened?" I asked, watching her.

The question seemed to snap her out of her shock. "I have to go home. *Now.*" She grabbed her purse that she'd discarded on the sofa, and dropped her phone inside, touching her palm to her forehead. "Oh my God. Maybe I should've had her call the cops now."

This wasn't the time to worry about my untended erection, not when she looked as close to falling apart as I had ever seen her. "What happened? Tell me."

In a shaky voice, she explained, "Somebody tried to break into my apartment. My sister is there. She fell asleep in the living room with the TV on. Maybe whoever it was thought the place was empty or everybody was asleep in their rooms. I don't know."

"Fuck. She should definitely have called the cops. But everything's fine, right?"

"I think it's something else." She was already on her way to the door, and I followed, stopping short when she did to keep from crashing into her. "Shit. What am I thinking? I need a ride."

Finally. Something I could do to help. "I can get you home."

It was like she didn't hear me, rambling, breathing fast. "She said some random guy tried to deliver food to the apartment earlier, and she brushed it off at the time. But now, she just remembered the guy used my name. He said it was a delivery for Rowan McNulty. I never ordered anything, obviously."

I was starting to understand what she meant when she thought this was about something else. "But he used your name? Did he say where he was from?"

"Did you hear me ask her that?" she snapped, shaking her head. "Sorry. No, she didn't know anything about it. But now she's wondering if maybe he was staking out the place before coming back. What if I have a stalker?" She was on the move again, leaving me trailing in her wake, following her to the elevator, where she jammed her finger against the button a few times.

My blood turned to ice. "Did she say anything else?"

"Only that he forced the door open, but the chain lock stopped him. He tried to break it, but she yelled, and he ran." She covered her face with her hands, and now sobs wracked her body. "What if he got in? What if he hurt her or took her? What if that's what he wanted?"

"Your sister?" Vaguely, I remembered Rowan talking about her years ago. She was a couple of years younger if my memory was correct.

"No. Not her. Oh my God. Do I need to find a new place? I need to get the locks fixed. Maybe we should stay at a hotel tonight," she mused as we stepped into the elevator car.

"I'm trying to understand. Does your sister live with you? If you need a place to stay, you could always spend the night with me. There's plenty of room. Whatever you need to feel safer."

"No." The firmness of her response surprised me, as did the way she quickly ran her hands under her eyes. She was determined to pull herself back together, so soon after falling apart. "That won't be necessary. But thank you."

What the fuck was this? All of a sudden, she was talking to me like I was a colleague instead of the man whose fingers were inside her minutes ago. "Why would you spend money on a hotel room when you're going to have to pay to have the locks fixed too? I'm only trying to help." She didn't need to act like I was the boogeyman. Like I was good enough to shove my fingers up her pretty cunt but not good enough to spend the night with if it meant feeling safe.

"Just... thank you for the offer, and let's leave it there. In fact," she continued as we stepped off the elevator in the lobby. "I can make it from here. Really, I'm so sorry to end the night like this. You don't need to worry yourself over any of it."

I had to be imagining things. No way was she walking to the exit rather than the garage, refusing my generosity and acting like there was anything normal about the past few minutes. "Wait. Dammit, why are you acting like this?"

"Please, Spencer. Trust me." She burst through the doors and onto the sidewalk, her head swinging wildly in a panic. "I'm going to get an Uber."

Instinct screamed in my head like a clanging bell, warning me there was something very wrong with all of this. "Like hell you are. I know you're hiding something. Why don't you want me to take you to your apartment?" Because that was the key. She didn't want me there. And whatever she was hiding, she didn't want to bring it to my place.

There was something close to hatred in her eyes when she shouted, "We're wasting time!"

"Fuck that. Tell me, then, instead of wasting time."

Her chin quivered, eyes searching my face. What was she so afraid of? "My daughter," she announced, resigned. "I have a daughter."

Not what I was expecting to hear. It changed things slightly, knowing she had a child, but who was I kidding? This was never going to go beyond tonight. It couldn't. I had a life to get back to, and so did she. Tonight was about sealing the deal, getting closure, and all that.

"So you have a daughter. And now you should definitely have your sister call the cops," I concluded, reaching for the phone in my pocket. "I'll fucking do it myself. What's the address?"

Before I could dial 911, though, something stopped me. Now that my erection had gone down, there was more blood flow to my brain, which was probably why it took so long for me to get what Rowan was determined not to tell me. Why would she not mention having a kid in the hours we'd spent talking over dinner? To be fair, it was none of my business.

My mind worked overtime. Unless there was a reason to keep her a secret? And where was the daughter's father? "How old is she?" I whispered while the traffic noise faded to silence, thanks to the blood now rushing in my ears.

Her flushed face went pale. "What difference does it make?" She wanted to fight. Her mouth worked, her features pinching together in something between anger and pain.

Her phone rang again, and she fumbled her way through getting it out of her purse. "Hello?" she breathed out, closing her eyes and pressing her fist to her mouth before speaking again. "Hey, baby. I'm on my way, okay? Everything's going to be fine."

The voice on the other side of that call was clear, loud, and raised in fear. This was not a baby, not a toddler. I didn't know much about kids, but I wasn't completely clueless.

By the time she ended the call and her shoulders sagged, I knew the truth. The rushing turned into a roar as the truth settled into my bones and vibrated through me, stealing my breath and clenching my stomach. I was a father. All this time. "If it didn't make a difference, you would tell me. Dammit, Rowan. How old is she? She's mine, isn't she?" I asked though I didn't need to. I only needed her to say it. I needed her to admit what she'd been hiding.

Something caught her attention further down the street. She darted toward the curb, waving an arm overhead to flag down an approaching cab, making me follow her. "Tell me!" I shouted, ignoring curious people passing on foot in favor of standing between her and the cab, which slowed to pick her up.

Tears shone in her eyes, on her cheeks, yet her voice shook with anger. "We don't need you. Understand? I'm handling this without you. The way I always have."

The truth in her words was a slap to the face, taking some of the wind out of me as she marched past and opened the cab's rear passenger door. I had two choices. Either hold her back with witnesses all around us or let her go. There really wasn't one to be made. There was nothing to do but stand there, watching as she jumped in and slammed the door.

But not fast enough. Not before she barked out the address of her apartment building to the driver. I made a note of it in my phone, then marched back into the lobby, this time walking straight through to the garage where my Bentley waited.

If she thought she could keep what was mine away from me, she never knew me at all.

She would after tonight.

8

ROWAN

"Please, can you go faster?" I knew the answer was no. The cab driver couldn't risk getting pulled over, or worse, because some weeping, shaking wreck of a woman begged him to floor the gas pedal.

I sank back against the vinyl seat, covering my eyes with one trembling hand. The truth was out. He knew. What happened next? I couldn't worry about that when it took everything in me not to throw up what little dinner I managed to eat earlier. What if that guy had gotten in without being scared off?

What if he...

Stop it.

Playing 'what if' was a waste of time. Hannah was fine—a little shaken up after she heard her aunt shouting in the living room, but she had been tucked in bed with the door closed when everything happened. She was only upset now because Rhiannon was upset. Things could have gone a lot worse.

Calling the police when I wasn't there would only make her more upset. I had to believe I made the right choice as the cab pulled to a stop in front of my building. I rushed through paying before bolting from the car and running for the entrance, taking the stairs to the fifth floor rather than waiting for the elevator. My baby was up there, and she needed me. I had already wasted enough time with Spencer.

"It's me," I called out between ragged breaths after knocking on the door. Rapid footsteps sounded on the other side, the chain slid, and the door opened.

"Mommy?" Hannah was wide-eyed, her long hair a little mussed from bed as she ran for me, holding out her arms. I dropped to my knees before she crashed into me hard enough to almost knock me over, burying her face in my neck. "I was so scared."

"I am so sorry that happened, sweetheart. You're okay. Everything is all right now." My sister, meanwhile, was biting her nails, shifting her weight from one foot to the other as she watched us from in front of the window overlooking the street. She had been looking for me.

"What should we do?" she whispered while I rocked Hannah and tried to see my way through the tangle of thoughts, fears, and questions bouncing around inside my skull. *What if... who was he... was he coming back...*

One thing was obvious. "I don't think you should spend the night here, sweetie," I whispered in Hannah's ear, stroking her back. Her tiny hitching breaths were painful to hear. "I can't get the door fixed until morning, and I wouldn't feel safe with you here if I can't lock it."

"But then you won't be safe," she whimpered, clinging to me.

"I'll be just fine. I'm going to call the police and make a report, and then I'm going to have to be here first thing in the morning for the repairman. I'm going to look up alarm companies, too, and have a system installed. We're going to be so safe here. Don't you worry."

Looking at Rhiannon, I asked, "Can you take her to Mom and Dad's?"

"Of course." She looked relieved now that she

had a definite plan and jumped into action, grabbing her purse and phone.

"You can come back tomorrow," I promised Hannah, kissing her forehead and cheeks, which tasted slightly salty. She'd done a lot of crying. My poor, sweet baby.

"Come with me," Hannah begged while fresh tears swam in her big, blue eyes. God, she looked so much like Spencer sometimes. It was hard to breathe, especially now when he was more than a memory. His face was clear in my mind's eye, making it obvious that she shared his nose and chin. The same little lines appeared between her eyebrows when they came together in confusion or frustration.

"I promise I will see you in the morning," I whispered, tucking her hair behind her ears. "I'll come and pick you up myself just as soon as the door is fixed, and we'll spend the whole day together. So long as I know you're safe in bed, I'll be just fine."

"Come on, sweetie." Rhiannon squeezed Hannah's shoulder. "I'll stay over too. We'll make pancakes in the morning."

What a time for jealousy to stir in my gut. I should have been the one making pancakes with my daughter in the morning. Somebody had to be here, though, and the property manager had a tendency to go MIA on the weekends. I couldn't trust anybody but myself.

"I'll see you in the morning. I promise." I kissed her cheeks again and forced a smile along with false warmth and enthusiasm in my voice. She ran a hand under her nose but begrudgingly put on her shoes and got her backpack from her room.

"I don't like leaving you here alone," Rhiannon whispered. "What if he comes back?"

"He'd be stupid to come back tonight, whoever he is." Besides, I knew something she didn't know, something Hannah didn't know. I wasn't about to take any chances—she was a smart, responsible kid, but plenty of responsible kids had ended up injured or worse by guns kept in the home. Mine was in the safe in my bedroom closet, where it had sat ever since I purchased it. I hated the idea of ever having to use it, but that was why it existed.

Letting her go felt a lot like ripping my heart from my chest. I pushed my way through it, waving at them as they left and walked down the hall. Once they disappeared into the elevator, I released the breath I was holding, slumping against the door frame, whimpering now that I was alone. Knowing how worried Hannah would be called up a real, burning pain in my chest.

I had to pull it together. Considering I didn't have the first clue about the specifics of the situation, calling the cops felt like a wasted effort. They might even be annoyed with me for wasting their time, not that it was my problem, but I didn't trust myself to be graceful in the face of rude, ignorant cops. I settled for using the chain lock again, then wedging one of the kitchen chairs under the doorknob.

I wouldn't get a minute of sleep in my room tonight. Instead of trying, I made a bed on the couch, then headed for the bedroom again to get changed. I took my phone with me, waiting for Rhiannon to let me know they had made it home safe.

By the time a message came through, I was in a pair of pajamas and washing the makeup off my face. I quickly rinsed off and reached for the phone, hoping to talk to Hannah before she went to bed for the second time tonight.

It wasn't Rhiannon.

My insides went cold when I saw Spencer's text.

Spencer: *I'm outside the building, wondering what else you've kept from me. Considering going door-to-door to find you. Unless you want me to piss off your neighbors, tell me your apartment number.*

"You stupid fucker," I whispered. Who was I talking to? Me or him? Because I was the one stupid enough to entertain his questions out on the sidewalk. Then again, what was I supposed to do? Scream for help like he was harassing me? The thought had passed through my head—not something I was proud of. I was in the middle of panicking at the time.

At least Hannah was gone, leaving no chance of an unplanned meeting. I'd never intended for him to know about her, but now he threatened to piss off my whole building in an effort to learn more. There was part of me that wanted to call his bluff and invite him to go ahead. We would see how far he got until he gave up.

On the other hand, now that he knew, that left the door wide open for me to say the things I had held back all this time. He had the nerve to act like I robbed him of the chance to be with his daughter.

With trembling hands, I typed 502 and sent the message before talking myself out of it. He must have missed Hannah leaving, or else I would've gotten a text from Rhiannon to warn me. No way would he have done the smart thing and stayed in the shadows, and there wasn't a doubt in my mind he would've recognized his child on sight. If only she didn't look so damn much like him.

I didn't have to wait long, and he was knocking on the door, making me wish I hadn't gone to that damn event for Alexander Landry. Since there was no turning back time, I took a few deep breaths to steady myself and moved the chair, unhooking the chain.

The way he pushed into the living room, anyone would think he was coming in to wage war. "Where is she?" he growled out, his head swinging back and forth.

"Are you fucking serious right now?" I closed the door and leaned against it, shaking my head at his theatrics. It was pretty pitiful. "For one thing, who do you think you are? This is my home. You don't get to barge in here and make demands."

"You lied to me." His teeth were clenched so tight I could barely make out a word he said. "You kept her from me."

"Kept her from you? Is that the story you're going with? You are truly deluded." Hell, maybe I should've thanked the creep who tried to break in here. The timing couldn't have been better. If it hadn't been for him, I would have fucked this asshole. There wasn't a doubt in my mind that was where we were headed before the phone rang. I would've had even more regret than I already did.

"What does that mean? What, you think I'm a liar like you?" His cold laughter slithered up my spine like a snake while we stared daggers at each other. "Not everybody is as good as you at only telling part of the story, Rowan."

"Enough of the bullshit, enough of the posturing. We both know you don't mean a word of it."

"What the hell are you talking about? What, do you think I'm pretending?" He laughed again, turning away, pacing to the window and back like a caged animal. "Right now, I wouldn't throw you a lifeline if you were drowning."

That was uncalled for, and it only added fuel to my burning rage. "You can leave my apartment if that's how you feel. Nobody talks to me that way, especially not somebody who has got to be a goddamn sociopath. How can you stand there and make me the bad guy in all of this?"

"Rowan! You had my baby, and you never told me you were pregnant!" He threw his arms into the air, his voice echoing when he raised it to the threshold of a shout. "You kept her a secret from me for more than ten years. I'm supposed to feel generous right now?" There was no time to process this before he whirled on me again, pointing a finger. "But no..." he continued, ignoring the way my mouth fell open, "...it's worse than that. You had every opportunity to tell me the past few days that I had a daughter in the world somewhere. How can you look me in the eye, knowing that, and still refuse to tell me about her? Doesn't she deserve to know who her father is?"

Something was wrong. Now that it was just the two of us in an otherwise quiet apartment, and I knew nobody was coming over here to attack my baby, I could focus on not only what he said but how he sounded.

How he looked.

He wasn't acting.

I had seen more than enough of it, good and bad, over the years to tell the difference. He was hurting. I had hurt him.

Somehow, that was the worst of all he had—the nerve to turn himself into a victim. Like he had been abandoned. "You know what?" I whispered, shaking with rage that was just beginning to simmer below the surface. "Maybe if you hadn't taken the coward's way out after the fucking crash that upended my whole goddamn life, you would've known about her."

"Wait—"

Yeah, fuck that. I was on a roll. "Maybe if I felt like I could trust you not to run away like a bitch the way you did, you might have watched our daughter grow up. And maybe if you didn't have me sign a contract stating I would never, under any circumstances, contact you ever again, I would have reached out. Do you think I wanted this? It's only by the generosity of my parents and my sister that I was able to make anything out of my life after you destroyed it. They're the reason Hannah has anything close to a semblance of normalcy. I could never have done it by myself, even with the damn money you threw at me."

By the time I got it all out, my chest was heaving, like I had just gone five rounds with the heavyweight champ. There was a feeling of pride that went along with it. Finally, I told him everything he needed to hear, and it felt so much sweeter than I had ever imagined because I hadn't imagined him having the nerve to act like he was hurt by the consequences of a choice he made.

I waited for him to react, expecting a firestorm of accusations and empty self-defense. When all I got was open-mouthed silence, I groaned. "Say something, at least. For once, take responsibility for your choices."

"Rowan..." He sounded for all the world like a man who had woken up from a long nap and didn't know what day it was or whether it was morning or night. A fuzzy sort of confusion was heavy in his voice, in the way he looked at me. "Exactly what did the contract say? Because I never read it."

"Oh, give me a break," I growled out, driving my heel against the door behind me with a grunt. "Like he wouldn't tell you."

"Who?"

"That ghoul. The lawyer." The thought of him made me shudder the way I would if a snake slithered over my foot.

"Jarvis?" he asked.

"Whatever. He didn't bother telling me his name. I told him I was pregnant... they did a test as soon as they admitted me and broke the news as soon as I was conscious. He showed up not long after that, totally out of nowhere, holding a document in front of me, telling me I was never allowed to talk about the accident."

Suddenly, he was very interested in the floor, staring at it as he muttered, "So I heard from my father, but only after the fact. I only knew about you agreeing not to go public with the accident. I swear."

"And I'm sure you and your dad high-fived before you both moved on. Because to people like you, all it takes is a payoff. Throw enough money at a problem, and you can sit back and relax, right?"

He searched my face, almost frantic. "But you told him? You told him you were going to have a baby?"

"The whole part where I was supposed to forget you existed made me figure I should say something. How was I supposed to never contact you when I was going to have your child?"

"What did he say?" I rolled my eyes, then flinched when he barked out, "Tell me! What did he say when you told him?"

"Let me see." I pretended to probe my memory like there was a chance of ever forgetting the tall, thin man's cruel words. Lowering my voice until it was almost as deep as the lawyer's, I said, "Let's not pretend girls in this town don't know how to solve an inconvenient problem." And even now, the memory of his cold, unaffected reaction chilled me. It just didn't matter to him, like he wasn't human.

"Rowan." I watched, wary, as he touched a hand

to his chest and swayed a little before getting a hold of himself. "Fuck me, Rowan. I had no idea."

"I..." The fact that the same word kept coming up made me ashamed of myself, tightening my throat until I pushed through. "I assumed you assumed I didn't go through with the pregnancy."

His head swung back and forth, the motion full of distraught. "I didn't know. I also had no idea this whole thing hinged upon you never seeing me again. I'm fucking serious," he grunted out when all I did was snort, derisive. "I didn't know. All this time..."

He sank onto the sofa, bending forward with his elbows on his knees and lowering his head into his hands. "I'll kill that son of a bitch. If he were in front of me now, I would. I thought... it was because you hated me for what I did. I thought you blamed me. You had every right to. I didn't know they forced your hand. I swear to God, I didn't."

I didn't want to believe him. It would've meant having believed so much that wasn't true all this time. I didn't want to think I had been wrong. But was it better to think he had really sat back, fully aware that he was cutting me out of his life forever? That he didn't care about the pregnancy?

I crept closer to him, an inch at a time. What was more surprising? That I wanted to comfort him, or how intense that desire was? Of all people, he was the last who deserved to be comforted, but was that true? Or was it only a story I had told myself?

By the time I stood in front of him, compassion took the place of suspicion. I reached out, tentative, and placed a hand on the back of his lowered head. He was quick to clasp my hand, closing his fingers around it and lifting his gaze. "I didn't know," he murmured. "All this time, I didn't have the first idea. I am so sorry I wasn't there for you. For both of you. You have to believe me."

I understood now how little I'd wanted to believe he could leave me like that. Deep down, I must have harbored a secret hope, or why would relief be washing over me now that he held my hand so tight, his eyes searching mine like he was looking for forgiveness?

"You are so beautiful." I barely processed what he said before he was on his feet, pulling me close and taking my face in his hands. He was so over-whelming, filling my senses, making my head spin until all I could do was lean against him for support while he lowered his head, touching his lips to mine in the softest kiss that threatened to stop my heart.

It wasn't soft for long. All at once, it intensified the way it had back at his apartment. I was as defenseless against him now as I was then, as I always was. I never could resist the power he had over me. What he did to my body, lighting me up, making me sizzle, tingle, and feel alive. When was the last time I felt this alive? I twisted his hair around my fingers while our tongues danced and my heart sang. He didn't mean to desert me. He didn't know.

Did it change anything?

I wasn't sure.

The only thing I was certain of was how much I needed him by the time he backed up against the sofa and dropped onto my makeshift bed. I followed him, straddling his lap, arms around his neck as I picked up where we left off and kissing him hard enough to make my lips sting. The touch of his hands up and down my back and over my ass was the sweetest fire, and in no time, I was rocking my hips, grinding against him until he groaned into my mouth.

The sound was an aphrodisiac, not that I needed one. I wanted to hear it again and again all night. I was working toward that when I ran my hands over his chest, slowly unbuttoning his shirt. He groaned again, his fingers sinking into my ass cheeks and drawing me in against what was so hard. Demanding. I was already wet, but now my pussy flooded, my clit aching. It had been so long since anybody touched me this way, and nobody had ever touched me the way he did. Even back then, when we were both so young, thinking we had all the answers.

He yanked the shirt free of his waistband and almost tore it off, then ran his hands under my nightshirt. Every touch left me wanting more. I was panting, lost in sensation and desire.

I lifted my arms, and he pulled the shirt over them, barely taking time to toss it aside before his hands took hold of my breasts. "Mmm... yesss," I moaned out, arching my back to give myself to him —all of me. I wanted him to take all of me, to make me forget any time had passed. To take the fire he had set in my core and share it with me until it consumed us both.

His thumbs worked my nipples, his tongue brushing against them. Back and forth, the sweetest torture. I realized the sharp, animal breathing I heard was coming from me as my hips ground against him furiously, already so close, beyond the point of caring how it looked to lose it like this. Not when I was sure the pain of my swollen clit would kill me if I didn't come soon.

"If I put a hand in these shorts..." he whispered

between licks against my sensitive nipples. "Would you be wet? Would that sweet pussy be all wet and ready for me?"

"Yes!" I gasped, lifting myself off his lap so he could do what he promised. He slid a hand between us, shoving it inside my soft cotton shorts and the thong underneath them.

Fireworks exploded at the slightest touch of his fingertips against my shaved mound. My teeth sank into my lip, barely muffling a scream as a massive orgasm slammed into me all at once. My nails scraped his muscular shoulders, and my body went stiff as the wave broke and I crashed against him, my breath moistening his skin when I buried my face in his neck.

"Shit," he whispered, his fingers still stroking my lips, teasing me as I trembled and whimpered. Slowly, he worked his way deeper, sliding through the river my slit had become. "More. I need more, baby. Can you come for me again?"

What had only started subsiding began to grow again—it was his voice, the growl running underneath it, his skillful touch. My hunger woke again, and soon, I was running my tongue over his neck and earlobe, moaning into his ear when he drove his fingers inside me.

"That's right," I whispered, moving with him, fucking his thick digits. "Make me come again. Make me come for you." He shuddered, hooking them against my G-spot while using his thumb against my clit until I was sure my sanity was going to shatter. My body jolted like a shock ran through it, so intensely it scared me. I wanted to run away from it, but instead, I held on, gripping him tight and giving over to the building tension.

This time it built more slowly, expanding in my core, filling me. "Let it go," he growled out close to my ear, breathing as hard as I was. "Let it go for me."

I didn't just let go. I exploded, bliss radiating through my limbs, stars dancing behind my eyelids. It was all-consuming, like nothing I had ever known, leaving me hanging between laughter and joyful tears. I was still coming down from that incredible high when Spencer laid me on my back.

"I'm going to need a taste of this." His deep, guttural growls sent shivers racing through me, ending at my already quivering pussy which he exposed after yanking down my shorts and thong. But it was the sight of him settling between my thighs that made fresh juices flow from my core. The look in his eyes—he was an animal, hungry. Greedy for me.

And when his tongue touched my slit, and he groaned like a starving man in front of a feast, I could've wept for joy. God, how had I forgotten how good he was at this? How eager and determined he was to make me come? There was a difference between a man going down on a woman because he felt he should and one who did it because he wanted to.

And Spencer Collins wanted to.

He paused only long enough to murmur two words. "So sweet..." Then his tongue was on me again, delving deep, parting my folds and sweeping through them, undoing me a little at a time with every lick, groan, and flick against my sensitive clit.

I opened my eyes to look down at him, lost in a fog of pleasure, and found him gazing at me from across the length of my body. Our eyes locked, and the tension ratcheted up until I fell back again, writhing, lost in the magic he was creating with his tongue. "I could do this all night." He sighed, parting my lips with his fingers to lavish my aching bundle of nerves with quick, light flicks that sent me hurtling over the edge and into oblivion.

How much more of this could I take?

I was ready to find out by the time he stood next to me, taking off his shoes, wasting no time dropping his pants. There was a wet spot on the front of his boxer briefs just beneath the head of his rigid dick. I'd forgotten how big he was, how good he felt inside me. My heart hammered with anticipation and gave me the guts to sit up and brush his hands aside in favor of pulling his shorts down myself.

"Put it in your mouth," he grunted out, taking his thick shaft in his hand and guiding himself to my waiting mouth. I ran my tongue around his head, and he sucked in a sharp breath while I sampled the salty precum. This was always my favorite—controlling his pleasure, setting the pace, deciding how hard to suck, following his cues.

Right now, they were a little more deliberate. He placed a hand against the back of my head and almost fed himself to me, fucking my mouth until I struggled not to gag. "That's right. Suck my cock good," he whispered, moaning softly, sounding like a man in the throes of ecstasy. My hands traveled over his thick thighs, up over his abs, until he pulled back with a reluctant sigh. "You're gonna make me come if you keep that up. And I'm not finished with you yet." The growl running through his words left my skin tingling.

I stretched out again, spreading my legs, my pulse picking up speed again at the way Spencer stared at my wet, pulsing pussy. "Gorgeous," he whispered, his eyes fixed on it while unrolling a condom over his dick after pulling it from his pants pocket. For a few moments, it was enough for him to watch me run my fingers over my lips, inviting him, getting off on the power I had over him.

But the power soon shifted when he kneeled between my thighs and dragged his head through my wetness. A brief flash of apprehension hit me. He was so much bigger than my memories, but I took a deep breath and forced myself to relax when the pressure at my entrance turned to blistering pleasure once he pushed his way inside me.

Fuck. Every inch of him stretched me in the best way, filled me, and made me claw at his bulging pecs and strong arms as sheer pleasure took over. His handsome face tensed like he was concentrating, savoring the moment, or maybe fighting off the impulse to come then and there. "Goddammit. How are you so tight?" he groaned out, clenching his jaw in determination. "Still pulsing. Trying to milk me. Have you missed my cock that much?"

The moment passed, and then he began to move, driving me a little closer to oblivion with every slow, deep stroke. He took his time, easing us into it. "Gotta go slow," he whispered, moving an inch at a time, torturing me, torturing both of us. His abs flexed in time with his agonizingly slow strokes, taking me a little further each time he slid in deep, building the tension.

"You feel so good," I whispered, resisting the impulse to beg him to fuck me hard. Fast. I didn't want it to end. Not ever.

"So do you. So... fucking... good..." His eyes closed as his teeth gritted, and he groaned from the strain of holding on. "You think you've got one more in you? Can you come on my cock?"

I didn't just think I could. It was inevitable, the tension building with every grunt from him, every moan, the breath that came quicker, shorter.

"Come with me," I begged, breathless, helpless against what was happening. He nodded slightly, picking up speed until he was pounding into me, almost frantically pumping in and out, losing his rhythm in favor of chasing his high. I followed him, jerking my hips, meeting every stroke until there was nothing for me to do but scream in pure, elated relief.

"Rowan... oh fuck!" I opened my eyes to watch him throw his head back, the tendons standing out on his neck, his skin flushed as he trembled from the force of his release.

And I already knew it wouldn't be the last time.

Slipping out of me, a shudder ran through me at the loss of him, but I was quickly distracted as I watched him disappear down the hall to the bathroom. Completely sated, I closed my eyes, trying to keep the barrage of questions I had from ruining the moment.

It wasn't until I felt him slide in next to me that I opened my eyes to meet his—a little hazy, a little unfocused, and I couldn't stop the small smile spreading on my face when he asked the last thing I expected to hear in a moment like this. "What's her name?"

Somehow, it was perfect. My heart swelled, and I grinned wide before whispering, "Hannah. Hannah Grace."

And when he smiled, I came dangerously close to falling for him all over again.

9

—————

SPENCER

Life looked a lot different on Monday morning.

I had flown down to Beverly Hills last week as an unattached bachelor—no commitments beyond my business, living a life of routine, enjoying myself whenever I could, basking in the trappings of my success. Such as the jet that had carried me home Sunday afternoon.

After the door was fixed, I was satisfied leaving Rowan alone to pick up Hannah and try to salvage what was left of the weekend. *"I have things I need to handle back home, but I'll be around soon,"* I'd promised. Whether or not it made a difference, I still didn't know. It seemed she prided herself on getting through without me. Not that I blamed her. She'd had plenty of practice.

"Mr. Collins? Everything all right?"

I didn't realize until my assistant called me out that the thought had made me growl. "Sorry, Viv," I offered. "What was that you were saying?"

She gave me a wary look. "Only that the security specialist you've been working with called your direct line before you got in earlier. He said you can call him back anytime for an update."

Security specialist. She was talking about Bruce Lewis, a former detective and current private investigator working with me on the Damian problem. It was he who'd tipped me off about the origins of the arsons in the Silicon Valley area and helped me tie them to the arson back in East Hampton. He always had an ear to the ground, reaching out to his vast network to track Damian and his thugs.

"Thank you," I told Vivian as we wrapped our catch-up session. "I'll call him right away. Remind me... when are my parents supposed to make it back from their trip?"

She frowned, squinting. For a woman old enough to be my mother, she had a hell of a sharp memory. "Next Thursday, I think? I can set a reminder in your calendar."

"No need. I'll remember." Because now, nothing would stop me from visiting my father face-to-face once he got home from his Mediterranean tour. It was something I usually tried to avoid, but this was not a typical situation.

It wasn't that I was surprised by what he did, exactly. I'd had more than a day to go over it from every angle. Of course, he would send that slimy lawyer to Rowan's hospital room just as soon as they were able to draw up an agreement. Taking advantage of an injured, scared girl without a moment's regret.

How did I know that? Because I knew the old man. I knew how ruthless he could be. I'd learned about more than just data analytics and algorithms in the two years I spent in China. Yet another reason I had no interest in working for him another minute once I came home.

It never crossed my mind that he would use that same ruthlessness against anyone I cared about. There I was, thinking I was beyond that level of naivete. He had proven me wrong, the bastard, and he was going to pay for it.

My first call of the day was to Bruce, who picked up on the second ring, sounding as gruff as ever.

"How was Beverly Hills?" he asked, forgoing a greeting.

"Illuminating," I replied since neither of us had the time to get into it. "What do you have for me?"

"I've heard our friend is pissed off that we got the jump on him when it came to the smear campaign against Miles Young."

I did like starting the day with good news. "Is that why he gave up so easily?" I asked because, as far as I could tell after scouring social media, the whole thing had fizzled out without much fanfare. Yes, the information was out there, but so was a statement from the family of the guy Miles had drawn into a fight. They were adamant that they didn't blame Miles and, in fact, thanked him for covering their son's medical bills all these years. Miles came out of it looking like a hero, and I hope he knew it. I hoped he would lie on the beach with his bride and put it behind him for now.

"He doesn't realize who he's fucking with this time around," I grunted out, imagining Damian's rage after going so far out of his way to sabotage us. "Do you have anything on those two employees he poached? I would think they've been laying low."

"You are correct," he confirmed. "I have a theory about that if you'd like to hear it."

"By all means."

"It's pretty simple. He paid them enough that they were able to disappear, both for his sake and for theirs."

Shit, I'd assumed that from the beginning. "They'd better hope I never catch up to them, or they're going to learn what happens to people who break an NDA."

"I'm going to keep looking. There's no way to really disappear in this day and age. There's always a trail. Unless..."

"Unless what?"

"Unless he silenced them permanently."

Right away, I wanted to dismiss the idea, but that would've been a mistake. I couldn't afford to think like a normal person now. I had to think like Damian, the sort of sick fuck who would burn down a dress shop or an office out here just to send a message. Something told me he wasn't too concerned about collateral damage if it meant getting what he wanted.

Bruce promised to keep me in the loop as we ended the call, leaving me staring out my office windows overlooking the bay. Normally, the sight of the sparkling water and the boats bobbing gracefully on it had a soothing effect. I'd always loved the water.

Even that didn't have the power to silence the overturned beehive my brain had become. My daughter was an hour's flight from where I sat, in school, by now. Who was she? Was she anything like me? Did she know anything about me? To think, a week ago at this time, I didn't have the first idea she existed.

I didn't have to care. That was the thing I'd spent most of Sunday reminding myself. Rowan hadn't asked for help, just the opposite. She didn't need me. Nobody was twisting my balls, forcing me to give a shit or acknowledge the kid as mine.

Did I want to acknowledge her? Did I want any of this?

What I wanted more than anything was a drink. Considering most people were just now sitting down at their desks for the first time all day, it would be best to wait until tonight. It occurred to me that my closest friends were in town at the same time, something that rarely happened.

I sent a text, inviting them out for drinks later on. It had been too long since the four of us had caught up, and I needed normalcy after days of anything but.

"WHEN'S THE last time we had a moment like this?" Lex looked around at the group and raised his glass, grinning. "Let's thank Spencer for getting us together for drinks when he realized we were all in town."

"No applause, please," I murmured, inclining my head while everyone laughed.

Clayton Manning tested his drink, snickering. "They call this an old fashioned?" he asked with a smirk, holding up the glass to examine its contents. "And people ask why I pay for my bartenders to attend training classes."

Nothing was ever good enough for him, but then that was the attitude that made him ten times the success of anyone in his family. He and his two brothers had divided the extensive number of restaurants, bars, hotels, and resorts after their father's death, but only Clay had spun his inheritance into a legacy of his own. "I had dinner at your new location in West Hollywood on Saturday," I told him. "You did well."

"Oh, so that was you." When I arched an eyebrow, he explained, "There was chatter about a last-minute reservation made by a personal friend of mine and how it meant pissing off the guest who already had that time reserved."

"You pay attention to shit like that?" Travis Knight laughed, slouching in his chair and loosening his tie. "I didn't know you were a micromanager."

"I pay attention to everything," Clay retorted, narrowing his dark eyes that glittered dangerously. "Nobody gets away with slacking off when they know the boss is watching."

"How do you have time to... well, do this?" Travis asked, touching his glass to Clay's before drinking deep. As if he wasn't just as busy, if not more, being stuck with his daughter once his ex-wife had decided to skip town. It meant his life was always hectic, though I would never have described himself as being stuck. Four-year-old Quinn was his little princess.

"Time management. You should learn about it." Clay snickered, making Travis groan while the rest of us laughed. We used to joke that he would be late for his own funeral, and stepping into the vice presidency of his family's shipping company hadn't trained him out of it. He was the sort of person who needed four alarms in the morning.

"So..." I caught the way Lex winked at the others,

then turned his attention to me. "How did things go with Rowan? Is she who you took to Clay's new restaurant to show off?"

"Rowan? Who's that?" There was curiosity in Clay's question, along with a knowing snort that told me my friends expected the typical story. Meeting a woman, getting into her panties, rinse and repeat. The same tale we'd been sharing with each other from those early days when I first met Clay and Lex at school to years later in China when Travis worked at the desk across from mine as a favor between our fathers.

"Somebody I knew years ago," I explained. "I happened to run into her while I was babysitting at an awards luncheon last week."

"Fuck off," Lex fired back, laughing. "*Babysitting.* You're so full of shit."

"Last I checked, you asked me to come along to keep you from either falling asleep out of boredom or drinking too much out of boredom and getting handsy with the wrong girl. Go ahead and tell me I'm wrong," I challenged, knowing he couldn't.

"Did you close the deal or not?" he settled for asking.

I'd done more than that. I found out I'm a father.

It was on the tip of my tongue—the looks on

their faces would be worth it. Instead of blowing their minds and facing a hundred questions, I settled for a shrug. "We caught up over dinner. That's it."

Lex sighed. "I'm disappointed, but don't be discouraged. There's plenty of willing pussy around here tonight." He was speaking to me, but his attention was focused on a curvy blonde standing at the bar. "Hey, she looks a little like Rowan. You can get it out of your system with her."

I used to say things like that, didn't I? Hell, I still would have if our positions were reversed. It was easy to make an offhand, smartass comment when I wasn't the one going through shit.

Things were different now. The blonde did nothing for me. If it hadn't been for the constant distraction of memories throughout the day threatening to get me hard at a moment's notice, I might have wondered if my dick was still working.

The strangest feeling swept over me, making me shift uncomfortably in the leather club chair. My friends were unaware, looking around the room, sizing up their options for when it came time to take the party elsewhere. All I could do was think about Rowan.

What was she doing tonight? What about Hannah?

"Where are you going?" Travis watched with the others as I stood, patting my pockets to make sure I had everything.

"I forgot a call I wanted to make tonight. The patent," I added, since clearly they weren't satisfied with my excuse. Let them think it was about business.

"Fuck, I was hoping you'd have better news about that by now," Clay mused, swirling the ice in his glass harder than necessary. "That fucker. Some people would be doing the world a favor if they stopped breathing."

"You sure your studio doesn't have those mob ties it did back in the day?" Travis joked, nodding to Lex. "Maybe you could take care of this problem for our friend here."

"Sorry to disappoint you." Lex wasn't joking anymore. I watched his jaw tighten and his eyes narrow. "We don't fuck around like that in this day and age."

"It was a joke, man. Didn't mean to offend." Sometimes, Travis didn't know when to stop. It was almost enough to make me reconsider leaving when

I did, in case Lex decided to retaliate, but they were big boys and could handle themselves.

Besides, I needed to go. Suddenly, an activity I had come to look forward to and even rely on at times as an escape had become tedious.

I knew where I wanted to be.

I was barely outside when I placed the call to my pilot. "Last minute flight," I explained as I waited for the car. Another Bentley. When I found what I liked, I stuck with it. "I'm on my way to the hangar now." I paid him enough to be ready at a moment's notice, and he didn't sound surprised at the sudden announcement.

While flying back to Beverly Hills, I did a little research. Rather, I let Bruce do it for me, calling him once I was in the air. "I need you to find an address. It's in the valley. The name is McNulty." He called me back not fifteen minutes later with an address for a Mr. and Mrs. Charles McNulty, who had apparently lived there for more than three decades. I could hardly imagine living in the same place that long, but I was glad they had. It made this much easier.

Within the hour, I was on the ground, behind the wheel, after having my car brought to the hangar in advance. With the address in my phone's GPS, I drove to the valley for the first time in as long as I could remember. It was barely past nine by the time I arrived, turning down their street and noticing how quiet it was. Peaceful. That was good. I wanted her to live someplace peaceful. Her mother had grown up here, and she had turned out pretty well, in spite of my interference.

The house in question was as modest as I had imagined. It couldn't have held more than three bedrooms on two floors and featured a small front and side yard, which I could observe once I parked a few houses down and across the street. A chain-link fence ran in front of it, but that was the only utilitarian feature. Somebody had painted the exterior a shade of yellow that was probably cheerful in the daytime, while the shutters were bright green. There were flowers in the front yard, plus potted plants on the porch. A pair of high-backed wicker chairs were out there, along with a swing big enough for two. There was a book sitting on the swing, and I wondered if my kid left it there.

I couldn't believe how much I wanted to go up there and find out which book it was—the smallest way to be connected to her.

I knew so many men my age, in my line of work, or at least wealthy and not looking to share that wealth with anybody. They would have shit their pants on the spot if they found out they had a kid. If the kid's mother told them not to bother trying to be involved, they would've gladly taken them up on it. It would have been like winning the lottery.

Not me. I didn't know that about myself until now. It was the sort of thing a person couldn't predict about himself, how he would react if the situation were more than hypothetical.

Somewhere in the little house, my daughter was living and breathing. Part of me existed outside my body. How could I not want to be part of her life?

How was I supposed to deal with her mother wanting nothing less?

My thoughts wandered as I drove away. A car like this would be spotted before long—minivans and late model sedans were more the speed around here. But I would be back.

Nothing would have kept me away.

10

ROWAN

When I was a kid, there was nothing better than Friday afternoon. School was out for the weekend, and there were two full days of freedom to look forward to. I had sort of lost that feeling as an adult, working my ass off seven days a week. Having Hannah with me on the weekends had brought the feeling back, leaving me feeling lighter and happier as we left Mom and Dad's the Friday after the close call with the intruder.

"Can we do something this weekend?" she asked with hope in her voice.

"Depends on what you had in mind." I carried Hannah's backpack by one strap while she carried a tote bag full of books, which Rhiannon had bought for her during a shopping spree at the local bookstore.

I hated to think how much she had spent, but I figured it had something to do with cheering Hannah up after last Saturday. Something to pick up her spirits, though she had seemed happy enough when we were together on Sunday after the door was fixed and Spencer had left.

Spencer who hadn't bothered reaching out since then. It shouldn't have come as a surprise.

"I don't know," she said, shrugging. "Anything. Maybe to a movie or something?"

Considering I would've asked to go to Disneyland when I was her age, I knew I was getting off easy even if ticket prices were a little ridiculous. "Sure, is there something you wanted to see?"

She opened the front gate and waited for me to pass before closing and locking it. Mom waved from the front door. She was a little concerned after the attempted break-in, but I had spared no expense with my new alarm system. Any breach resulted in a call going straight to the local police station. I also made sure the front desk staff was aware that they had let somebody upstairs without confirming an order had been placed. They were supposed to do that. The property manager made sure to tell me the girl working the desk that night would be dealt with. Considering she could've gotten my daughter hurt or killed with her laziness, I couldn't bring myself to feel sorry.

Blissfully unaware of my thoughts, Hannah shook her head, making the golden curtain hanging past her shoulders shimmer in the last beams of early evening light. "No, but there's probably something that wouldn't be too grown-up or whatever."

"I'll look into it." I stroked that golden hair, wrapping an arm around her and giving her a squeeze on the way to my car, parked a few houses down from my parents'.

"You don't have a date this weekend?" she asked, and I looked down, catching the sly look she gave me.

"Is that what this is about, young lady? No, I do not," I told her, sticking out my tongue. "So there."

It was a good thing she couldn't hear the way my heart sank. No, I wouldn't have a date, and there was absolutely no reason for any sadness because of that. Spencer and I had slept together once. Well, technically twice, but both in the span of a few hours. He had told me Sunday morning that he had a busy week ahead of him.

I had no right or reason to expect anything more

than that. He didn't need to call, text, or send an email. If anything, his silence might have been preferable to contact. He could have sent that scary lawyer after me, demanding a paternity test or forcing me to sign something saying I would never go after him for child support. When I thought of it that way, it was better that he faded into the background again.

So what if this felt way too much like history repeating itself? This time, he knew what he was missing out on. Nobody was lying to him, concealing the truth. He was making this decision on his own.

"It'll be just you and me this weekend, kid." And that was just fine. It was what I was used to. I opened the passenger door for her, and she loaded her books in the back seat after climbing in. Which meant she didn't see what I did. If she had, she wouldn't have known what she was looking at, anyway.

But I knew.

Did he think he didn't stick out like a sore thumb sitting in a Bentley on this block?

"I'll be right back. You stay here." I didn't wait long enough to hear Hannah's response and closed the car door. Now that I had Spencer in my sights, nothing was going to stop me from finding out what the hell was going on.

He stepped out of the car, holding his hands up in front of him. "Just listen," he said.

"No. You just listen," I snapped, caught between outrage and a strange sense of relief. "What the hell are you doing here? I hear nothing from you for days, then I find you sitting here? I thought you were back home."

"Is there anything wrong with me coming down to see her? Is that a crime?" Arching an eyebrow, he added, "You're the lawyer. Tell me."

"Don't even hand me that shit," I hissed. To think, I spent the week fighting to convince myself it would be a good thing if he ghosted us while my heart ached. Would I ever stop being a glutton for punishment?

"It's the truth. I wanted to see her. I didn't think you would want that, but I couldn't help myself. You can't expect me to forget she exists." The corners of his mouth tugged upward. "She's a beautiful kid. She looks just like you."

And there I went, melting into a puddle and soaking into the asphalt. Hearing him talk that way about her was something out of the sort of dream I never dared imagine coming true. I always wondered what he would think of her.

What the hell was I thinking? This was why things were better before we met up again. He always fucked with my head, whether or not he knew it.

I stood up straight, shaking my head. "No. You are not allowed to sit out here like some creepy stalker and freak her out if she notices. How could you?" It came out all at once, the words tumbling over each other. My heart was racing a mile a minute, and there was a roaring in my ears.

Dammit, why did he have to do this?

Lifting a shoulder, he retorted, "You're the one who came over here and made a thing about it. She didn't notice me all week."

I hated that he was right. It took a little of the heat out of my rage as I processed what he was saying. "All week?" My mouth fell open.

"There's a lot of time to make up for." Out of so much confusion, what confused me most was how mellow he seemed. Normally, he would meet my anger with his own shitty attitude. That was how it always was back in the day, and it wasn't like we hadn't antagonized each other recently.

"Either way," I whispered. "It's unacceptable." A

glance over my shoulder told me Hannah was waiting in the car, probably on her tablet. Right then, I didn't mind. I preferred the distraction.

"What is so unacceptable about wanting to see my daughter?" he asked.

His daughter. Damn my weak, stupid heart for fluttering when he said that. Damn me for being so easy to melt, especially when it didn't seem he was trying to melt me. There was nothing sneaky about his attitude. He wasn't being coy. He wasn't screwing with my head, even if that was how it felt. It was all my fault, wanting to give in like this.

"Maybe we could start with boundaries?" I suggested, getting myself back on track. We had to talk about the things that really mattered. "If you want to meet her, let's make a plan. Let's decide together what would be best for her. That's all I'm asking."

Yet another trait Hannah had picked up from him—the sly look so much like the one she gave me minutes ago. "So you're saying you want me to meet her?"

I didn't know what I was saying. Why did he sound hopeful? Did he mean it? "I'm saying don't hurt my kid. That's it."

"Mom?"

Oh, fuck me. Hannah's soft question made my insides shrivel like desiccated leaves. I turned and found her standing behind me, staring over my shoulder before her gaze flicked back to me. "Everything okay?" she asked.

I would hate him forever if he screwed this up. Putting on a smile, I said, "Fine, sweetie. Just give me one more minute, and I'll be with you."

She glanced at him again. What was she thinking? Did she notice the way her eyes mirrored his—sharp and piercing, with a hint of mischief lurking in the corners? Or the subtle curve of her lips that echoed his own. Did she know? Could she sense it? The silence twisted between us, and I held my breath, feeling the weight of the moment pressing down. That was almost too paranoid to be taken seriously, but it was a very real fear.

Smirking, she said, "You don't have to pretend."

I was going to die right there on the spot. It was painful to pretend everything was fine, but I managed to ask, "Pretend what? Nobody's pretending."

"You can introduce me to your boyfriend. Jeez." Her wide, wicked little grin both came as a relief and deepened the pile of shit I was sinking into.

"Sweetie, he's not... I mean, it's not..."

"I'm a friend of your mom." Somehow, Spencer managed to sound normal while I had forgotten most of the words I had ever learned. He stepped up beside me and extended a hand. "My name is Spencer. What's yours?"

"Hannah."

It was happening. She was placing her hand in his and shaking it, and they were smiling at each other. While it was nothing I had ever imagined, it healed something in me I didn't know was broken.

He played it off well, releasing her hand without holding on too long. "It is nice to meet you, Hannah. What's your favorite subject at school?"

His question took me by surprise, but she took it in stride. "English. I like the books we have to read."

"What are you reading now?"

"Hannah is in an advanced program," I explained, grinning with pride at my kid. "She's only ten, but she's reading at an eighth-grade level."

"Mom..." She groaned, rolling her eyes the way I used to when Mom and Dad praised me out of nowhere. I used to hate it, and now I was doing it to her. "We're reading *The Outsiders*," she explained.

"Good book. I read that when I was in school. I would like to know what you think about it." All of a sudden, he remembered I was standing next to him, glancing my way. "We could talk about it over dinner. What do you think? I'm in the mood for a burger." He eyed Hannah because, of course, he didn't know what kind of food she liked.

"Yeah, Mom! Can we?" Her eyes danced, her head bobbing in excitement.

We'd need to have a talk about putting me on the spot. This prick. He knew damn well I wouldn't be able to say no unless I wanted to look like the mean mom with a stick up her ass.

"Can I buy you a burger?" he asked, and I realized for the first time how his eyes gleamed the way hers did when he knew he was about to get his way.

"I'm outnumbered." I sighed, throwing my hands into the air. "You can follow us to the restaurant."

"I like writing stories." Hannah played with her straw, stirring around what was left of her milkshake. "Maybe that's what I'm going to do when I grow up."

"What kind of stories do you like to write?" Spencer sounded very solemn, but then he had throughout the meal. Not in a negative way, not like he was bored. Rather like he took her very seriously, the way a lot of adults didn't take children—he wasn't patronizing her. There were no sly winks my way.

Was it safe to believe he meant it?

And what would happen if he decided to announce who he was? What if he tried to take her from me?

I took a long sip of my milkshake in the hope of cooling myself down. I couldn't think that way. It would mean ruining what was turning out to be a nice night. I was witnessing my daughter get acquainted with her father, and all I did was worry.

Then again, it would've been naïve of me not to at least question his motives just a little. He kept calling her his, like she was a possession. I wouldn't let him get close to her just for the sake of ownership. She deserved better than that.

"Fantasy, mostly," she explained. "I'm working on one right now. I love making up places and creatures and characters."

"You know what I think? That is definitely what you should do when you grow up. It's something you like to do, and you sound excited when you talk about it." He turned to me. "What do you think?"

"Definitely," I agreed. At least we could agree on that much, even if I still didn't love his methods. I couldn't fault him for it when he and Hannah were getting along so well, and he seemed so genuinely interested in her.

Hannah turned her attention to me. "Like you wanted to be an actress?"

Out of the mouths of babes. It was an innocent question, and I knew it came from years spent around my old photos, not to mention a pair of grandparents who loved to tell their favorite stories. Just because I didn't make it a point to sit around and talk about the past didn't mean nobody else did.

I was aware of Spencer watching me as I figured out how to respond. "I did want to be an actress," I began, speaking slowly, choosing my words carefully. No amount of chocolate milkshake would make this any easier. "But things changed. That's how life goes sometimes. And as it turns out, I really like what I do now. It was always going to be either acting or law. I tried one first, then I went back to school and got my degree. I think it was the right thing to do."

She didn't see my scars the way other people did. She had never known me without them. They were part of me, so it never would've occurred to her that they were the reason I had to give up on that dream. Well, she was part of that reason, too, realizing I needed something solid in my life. I had responsibilities, and hush money didn't fall from the sky every day. I had turned down a scholarship, but tuition had come my way after all.

She was too young to understand all of that, but I planned on explaining it one day. And when I did, it wouldn't be in a restaurant full of people.

That was the thing. Her question wasn't as deep as I took it. She accepted my explanation and moved on. "Can I get dessert?"

Now, this, I could handle. "Excuse me, but what's that in your glass? Something to do with ice cream, right?"

Only a ten-year-old would look so stricken over something so trivial. "No fair! I didn't know it was either a milkshake or dessert. I would've picked dessert."

"Maybe we can share something," Spencer suggested. "Then it wouldn't be so bad."

So that was the kind of father he would be if he chose to be her father and not just the man who donated his DNA. I would be the voice of reason, and he would be the one scheming to get around my decisions.

I didn't even mind. In fact, I sort of liked the idea. It was easy to imagine us like this, the three of us together, going out for dinner on a Friday night, sitting around the table at home, or watching movies on the couch.

I needed to get real. Thinking like that would only lead to trouble. I was setting myself up for heartache. Not only mine, either. I wasn't going to welcome Spencer into our lives unless I knew for sure he wanted to be there.

That was why, as Hannah carefully decided what she wanted for dessert, I sent a text to the man sitting directly across from me in the booth.

Me: *We should talk. Come back to my apartment after this.*

11

SPENCER

Why did people think it was so hard to handle kids? Before tonight, I had all of five minutes of experience being around them, if that. The first meeting with Hannah should have been awkward. I should've been tongue-tied.

"Tell me the truth." Rowan left her purse sitting on the sofa and took off her heels, sighing in relief while Hannah went to her room to drop off her books and backpack, leaving us alone for a second.

With a glance down the hall toward Hannah's bedroom door to make sure we were alone, Rowan asked, "Have you been hanging out with kids all these years? Do you have a lot of friends with big families?"

"Not even close." I studied the alarm system keypad mounted beside the door, nodding in appreciation. "This looks good. Are the windows alarmed too?"

"Yes, of course." She let out a flat laugh behind me. "I should've done it sooner. Now, I have to remember to disarm it before opening the door. I doubt the LAPD would appreciate being called out here for nothing."

Her tap against my shoulder came as a surprise. She was damn silent in her bare feet. "So how the hell were you so good with her?" she asked when I turned around.

"When I was her age, I hated people talking to me like I was a dumb kid," I mused. "It was patronizing. So I talked to her like she was more grown-up, the way I wished somebody would talk to me."

"Very smart. She hates being talked down to." She then voiced a revelation before I had the chance. "She takes after you."

There was something humbling about that. A part of me existed in the world with the same tendencies. I could see a little of myself in her face too. The whole damn thing was unnerving, but not in a bad way. It was damn baffling.

Hannah called out from her room. "Mom! I'm

putting my pajamas on, but that doesn't mean I'm ready to go to bed." Yep, she was my kid. Always setting the rules.

"She does this every. Single. Weekend." Raising her voice, Rowan replied, "You're creeping up on bedtime. How about we compromise, and you read in bed until you get sleepy?"

"Okay!" The door opened, and Hannah poked her head out into the hallway. "Spencer, if I don't see you, thanks for dinner."

This was a great kid. Maybe I recognized how great she was because I was such a little shit growing up. I only hoped she didn't take after me in that respect. "You're welcome. Thanks for splitting that brownie sundae with me." I felt a little sluggish, but it was worth it.

"And if you end up with a stomach ache tonight," Rowan called out. "You can call Spencer and thank him for that too."

"Oh, Mom." Only a kid would roll their eyes and look so over everything. "I'm not a baby."

"She's got you there," I muttered, chuckling when Rowan shot me a dirty look.

Once things quieted down again, I sank into the sofa and had to resist the temptation to unbutton my pants. It had been a long time since I ate that much junk in one sitting. "So. What did you want to talk about?" I asked because I wasn't going to make this easy for her. Not after she damn near tore my head off earlier on her parents' street. It was one thing to have a surprisingly good time with my kid, but she was out of the room now, and the grown-ups had important things to discuss.

I knew she was regretting that text. She looked like she swallowed her tongue before retreating to the open kitchen, where I watched her puttering around, unloading the dishwasher and wiping the counter with a dish towel. It didn't look to me like it needed cleaning, but she seemed pretty intent on doing chores.

"Would it help if I made a mess for you?" I asked. "So you'll have a reason for all of that."

The moment a grin touched her mouth, I knew I had set myself up. "I think you've already made enough of a mess. Thanks so much," she murmured with a sweet, sarcastic smile.

Dropping the dish towel, she leaned on the granite counter with her palms. "I hope you don't think this is the kind of thing that's going to happen all the time. You randomly show up and suddenly, the three of us are spending an evening together."

Here we go. I was expecting this. A week of

thinking and planning had left me with an arsenal to use against her if need be. I only hoped there wouldn't be a need. "Why can't it happen?" I asked.

"Why do you want it to?" she countered.

"You can't mean that."

"I absolutely do." I opened my mouth to protest, but she held up a hand, "Listen to me before you start throwing your ego around. This is not some new hobby for you to become interested in. I'm not going to have you becoming part of her life and making her care about you, only for you to disappear when you get bored or something more interesting comes along."

Again, not surprising. If anything, she was more predictable than I expected. That didn't mean I wanted to hear her talk down to me like I was some slug. "I'm insulted you think I would do that."

"Here's the thing," she fired back in a loud, fierce whisper from the other side of the breakfast bar. "This isn't about you. It's not about what I think of you. It's not about our past. It's about looking ahead to the future, mapping out possible outcomes, and doing everything I can to prevent the shitty ones. So I have to say to myself, what's the worst possible way this might turn out? Then, I do everything I can as her mother to avoid it."

Glancing toward the hallway, she continued, "After watching her with you, the worst possible way this could turn out would be for you to show an interest in her and then walk away. It would be one thing if you did it right now because she doesn't know who you are. If you ever want her to know you, to really know you, you need to commit."

The only sound for a long time was that of her breathing. It must have taken a lot to get through that. I wasn't the only one who had done a lot of thinking lately. "Is that it?" I finally asked. "Because I've been putting plans together this week and thought you'd like to hear them since you're all about commitment. Nothing's set in stone. It's all completely flexible. I thought you would want to have a say in things."

"That's generous of you, giving me a say in things, but what are we talking about?"

"Financial planning," I explained. "A means of providing for Hannah for the rest of her life. I'd set you up as trustee, giving you the power to control her money until she comes of age."

What did I expect? Not profuse thanks. I knew better. Something more than the disdain she shot me, though. "Wow. That's not even remotely what I was talking about."

"Why do you have to sound so combative?"

"Why do you have to butt in where I didn't ask you to be?" She stepped into the hall and held up a finger, cocking her head toward Hannah's room. Exercising the superhuman hearing that seemed to come with being a mom.

Once she was satisfied it was safe to continue, she turned to me with her arms folded. "Well? Answer the question."

If she'd been grilling anyone but me, her attitude would've gotten me rock-hard. She was smoking hot even in bare feet, with a small ice cream stain on her pale green blouse. I pulled my attention from it and stood, hands on my hips. "A man has the right to provide for his kid. It's bad enough I only found out about her. You can't expect me to stand back and act like I don't know she exists. I'm going to provide for her."

Her lashes fluttered as she stammered, sounding a little softer when she spoke again. "I understand how you feel, and I appreciate it, but I can provide for her. I'm not exactly doing badly for myself."

Only reminding myself Hannah would be able to hear kept me from losing it. Why did she have to be so fucking stubborn? "Would you stop letting your pride get in the way? What's wrong with me wanting to set up a college fund for her?"

"You said trust," she pointed out. "Now we're talking about a college fund?"

"We're talking about whatever I say we're talking about," I growled out. Fuck being the bigger person. "Why wouldn't you want to give her the best possible start in life? I'm not asking for anything in return but knowing I gave her everything I could. Especially since..."

Arching an eyebrow, she asked, "Especially since what?"

"You never planned on telling her about me, did you?"

That got her. Her invisible barriers dropped. She touched a palm to her forehead before running her hand through her hair. The energy between us shifted, softened. "Spencer, until a week ago, I thought you deserted me. You hired somebody to draw up an agreement that guaranteed I would never bother you again. I mean, there's rejection, and there's a binding legal agreement. Can you understand why I wouldn't be in a hurry to tell Hannah all about the magic of how she came to be?"

Now that she put it that way, it seemed fairly obvious. "All right, point taken."

"And to be honest with you, I don't know that I want my daughter involved with a family where there are people capable of the sort of shit your father and his lawyer did to me."

"Let's get one thing straight." Her head snapped back at my sudden change in tone, but I wasn't about to apologize. She needed to understand. "He will *never* have anything to do with her. He was in such a hurry to pretend she didn't exist? Fine. He will never be fortunate enough to speak to her. Do you think I'm lying?"

"No." There was no hesitation. "I don't think you're lying. And I understand you wanting to put money aside for her, and I think that is a good idea. But understand me... this isn't going to be a tit-for-tat situation. You provide her college fund so that gives you leverage over me or like a louder voice when it comes to making decisions. Do you see what I mean?"

I did, and I was a little disappointed. This was a possibility I hadn't considered. That she might kick me in the balls or as good as. My pride stung as much as my balls would have. "You think I would do that?"

"How the hell would I know?" she whispered. "This is all new. Everything's changed. And yeah, we had six great months together, but that's all we had. I don't know you well enough to know what to expect, and..." she sighed as the fight drained from her, "...and I'm a little scared. I don't know what's going to happen. I guess I feel like I did at first, back then. Everything is new all of a sudden. I have to relearn the rules."

Her lips drew into a thin line as she turned away, wrapping her arms around herself and going back to the kitchen. I followed her into the spotless space. "Do you have somebody come in to do the cleaning?" I asked since it hardly looked like the room was ever used. It was that clean.

She looked around, letting out a soft laugh. "I clean when I'm stressed. I've been doing a lot of it this week."

Did that mean this clean room was thanks to me? I was about to ask the question when she shut the cabinet door hard, her head hanging low. "I was going to make tea, and I don't even have tea. What the hell is wrong with my head?"

"Hey. I know this has all been a lot." It had been a lot for me, too, but something told me she didn't want to hear it. Not with the way she was feeling. "But you don't have to worry. I'm not trying to take her from you. I'm not trying to outdo you or erase everything you have together. It's not like that."

"I want to believe you."

I hated how defeated she suddenly sounded. That was what scared her most of all—losing Hannah to me. I had to convince her that would never happen. It would make the difference between getting to provide for what was mine and being kept on the outside for the rest of my life.

Stepping up behind her, I touched my hands to her hips, leaning close. "You have nothing to worry about. I'm ready to take things slow. I do understand where you're coming from. You've raised a great girl."

"I wish I could take credit for her," she snorted. I couldn't help lowering my head to indulge in her hair's floral scent. Her head tipped back to touch my shoulder as she sighed, melting into me. "Sometimes, I wonder if I've had enough of an influence in her life. I've missed so much too. You're not the only one. I wonder if I'll spend my whole life trying to make up for that."

"Take it easy on yourself." It was natural, necessary to touch my lips to her ear, her jaw. I couldn't be this close to her without wanting more.

"There's never a time I feel like I have everything under control." She surprised me by chuckling softly while my lips skimmed her neck. "Wow, it actually feels good to be able to say that. I never felt comfortable enough to say it to my family."

I saw how that would feel good. I understood how isolated she must've felt all this time. No wonder she hated me so much during that first meeting when we went for drinks, and all I cared about was covering my ass. That was miles away now. Still important, but not nearly as much when compared to the woman my arms slid around.

"Spencer..." There was a mix of desire and warning in her whisper when my hand cupped her tit. Her nipple went hard under my thumb, and I ran in circles over the tight peak. "No fair. You know we can't do this. She's, like, feet away from us." Turning in my arms, she wrapped hers around my neck and smirked up at me. "And just because we slept together doesn't mean you automatically get access every time we're in the same city."

"Every *other* time?" I suggested, making her blurt out a laugh. She wasn't fooling me. This pretense of resistance was just that. The last gasps of whatever it was she thought she should do. Who she thought she needed to be.

"Fine, but not while Hannah is mere feet from where you're groping her mother." Her smile hardened into something fiercely maternal. "Hard boundary."

My dick was halfway to going rigid, and I would've loved nothing more than to be balls-deep in her, but I saw her point. "We have to get together on a weeknight," I decided, breathing her in again, pulling her essence into my lungs. It was the most I'd get tonight.

Nothing could have been sweeter than her smile. "Yes. We definitely do. You're not the only one with a craving," she purred, running lazy fingers through my hair and setting my blood on fire. That was all it took—the simplest touch, so long as it came from her.

"A craving?" I couldn't help groping her ass a little while she was still in my arms. "I like the sound of that. I'm something you can't shake."

Her hips shifted as she thrust her pussy against my growing bulge. "That's a good way of describing it. The kind of thing you know you should resist…" she grazed my lips with hers, making me groan and grind against her, "… but you can't," she concluded with a wicked grin that did dangerous things to organs other than my dick. My heart beat harder, faster, like something exciting was happening. Maybe it was.

It didn't have to mean anything. Whatever was happening between Rowan and me could be separate from Hannah and me. I would keep the lines from blurring.

"I guess I'll have to go home and jerk off." I sighed, pouting until she giggled.

"I have an idea." There was a wicked gleam in her eye as she bit her lip. Dear God, she was a drug. "Why don't I send you some inspiration for when you get home?"

"What did you have in mind?" I asked with a growl.

"Why don't you head out, and you'll see very soon?"

It wasn't easy, pretending to be scornful as I let her go and backed away. "I see what this is all about. You lure a man into buying you dinner. Then you get them out of the apartment by promising to send nudes? That's a unique hustle you have going on."

"Get the hell out of here." She laughed, turning me in place and pushing me toward the door. "And thank you for dinner."

"Thank *you*." I turned to her when I reached the door, taking her face in my hands. Instead of shoving my tongue down her throat the way instinct demanded, I settled for a soft kiss that ended before it could lead anywhere else.

I was behind the wheel in the garage when the first text came through from her.

Rowan: *Inspiration part one…*

And a photo followed.

"Fuck me." I groaned, my dick swelling at the shot of her tits in a see-through lace bra. Her nipples stood out and begged to be sucked through the fabric until she creamed her panties.

Rowan: *Part two.*

I held my ragged breath while waiting for the next image. This time, she'd hiked her skirt up to flash a bit of a lace thong. My dick jumped at the idea of what was coming next.

Another text.

Rowan: *Maybe I'll make myself come for you later. Maybe I'll let you listen while I do.*

At this rate, I might not be able to make it home before I had no choice but to fuck my fist with her name on my lips. "There had better not be traffic," I muttered, starting the engine and pulling out in a damn hurry.

12

———

ROWAN

ow is it only Thursday?

My gaze swept over the mess of contracts, notes, and headshots spread across my desk—prospective clients, so fresh-faced and full of dreams. There were times when looking at them made me more aware than ever of what set us apart. I had been that bright and full of hope back when I had my first headshots taken.

"First thing Monday morning, send onboarding materials out to Isabella along with a *welcome to the family* bouquet. Confirm the meeting at the studio next week to go over the final draft of her contract."

My assistant nodded, jotting down the instructions. Noelle was one in a million, able to predict my next thought before it even began to stir in my head.

"You also have the dinner with the Landry International people on Tuesday night. Are you confirming?"

"Yes, of course. I almost forgot. What would I do without you?" I asked. My head was just shy of pounding after days of back-to-back meetings, lunches, and dinners. Hollywood newcomers worried about their future, parents worried about their kids, executives wanted to be sure they were covered against any liability.

Those were the meetings that made me grind my teeth a little. It was a necessary evil, a means of creating and maintaining relationships with heavy hitters who could end up bringing me endless business in the future. But they weren't the people I was trying to help, to protect. I didn't get the same feeling of pride in my job after working out a deal with them.

"Do you have any plans with Hannah this weekend?" Noelle asked.

That I could talk about until I went blue in the face. "Nothing concrete, but I have a few ideas." Most of them revolved around the man who'd been sending texts all week, checking on me, asking if Hannah was doing all right, and finding out whether we could get together this weekend once he flew into town.

And I was basically fighting for my life, reminding myself with every text that came through and made my heart skip a beat that I was Hannah's mother, that I had to remove my personal feelings from the situation and keep her best interests in mind. That meant making sure not to get all wrapped up in his enthusiasm.

Thinking about Hannah jogged my memory. A few texts came in while I was on a Zoom call earlier in the morning, but I had been too busy to check. Once Noelle left my office, I opened the app to read what Spencer sent.

Spencer: *Does Hannah like baseball?*

Spencer: *A friend of mine has a luxury box with the Giants and is always offering his tickets. We can take my jet.*

Spencer: *Has she been to Disneyland?*

How was I supposed to guard either of us when seeing him so eager to please made my heart ache in the best way? I'd always hoped that if the day ever came, he would want to be part of her life.

Even so, one of us had to be intelligent about this.

Me: *I think Disneyland might be a little much at*

first. The jet too. Maybe we could settle for dinner and a movie? Work our way up?

Yes, I was essentially hinting at a future by saying that, but I didn't bother correcting myself before sending the message. She liked him, and he was clearly enamored with her. I didn't want to stand in the way.

I only hoped he wouldn't let me down.

More importantly, let her down.

A calendar alert chimed on my computer, reminding me of a lunch date with my sister. We hadn't spoken much in the almost two weeks since the break-in attempt. She was busy with her job, which was nothing new, but she sounded almost giddy when we made these plans.

"I have news for you," she had said a few days ago over the phone and refused to give me any details until we saw each other today. Even if I weren't half-starved after working through breakfast, I would've hurried through, grabbing my purse and taking a last-minute trip to the ladies' room before speed walking the two blocks to the café, where Rhiannon was already waiting at one of the tables set behind a low, decorative fence separating it from the sidewalk.

Right away, I noticed her gorgeous, trendy outfit. She looked like she had been shopping on Rodeo

Drive recently, something that had never interested her much in the past. Was she finally starting to spend her savings on herself? Her freshly blown-out hair and new designer sunglasses gave me hope.

"You look fantastic," I told her once I reached the table, kissing her cheek and sitting across from her. We ordered salads and iced tea. Then I got down to business. Why bother beating around the bush? There was an elephant in the room that needed discussion.

"Spill it," I demanded, folding my hands on the table, facing her the way I would face somebody in an important meeting. "What is it you wanted to tell me? I've been dying to find out."

"Now I feel dumb for overselling it."

"Don't do that," I warned with a shake of my head and my sternest big-sister scowl. "Don't act like you weren't practically jumping out of your skin when we decided to have lunch today. What's the big news?"

"I'm just saying, it might not be as big of a deal as I want it to be..." She chewed her lip, positioning her sunglasses on top of her head so I could get a look at the excitement in her eyes. "I'm seeing somebody. He's really great."

"That's amazing! It's about time, woman!" When

our iced teas were delivered to the table, I lifted my glass in salute. "No wonder you look like you just walked off a runway, girl. I'm going to need to know where you've been shopping."

"It's just been really nice." The joy in her smile was like sunshine after a storm. Rhiannon was beautiful, smart as hell, with an amazing heart. For some reason, she had a habit of looking down on herself. She didn't see herself the way we did, the people who loved her. She was a late bloomer, so it hadn't always been easy to find her place in the world. That sort of thing could stick with a person even when they were grown up.

"So what's his name?" I asked. "Tell me everything about him."

Her head tipped to the side. "Tell me who *you've* been seeing."

"No fair! I'm not seeing anybody, anyway," I reminded her.

She pursed her lips, eyes narrowing to slits. "That's not what Hannah told me."

"That little stinker. She is in so much trouble." I was all smiles and laughter on the outside, but internally? It was a different story. I quaked, going cold even in the brilliant midday sunshine.

"So you admit you've been lying to me, and you

are seeing somebody." She was enjoying the hell out of this, riding high on the adrenaline rush of a new boyfriend. So what if I was dying inside?

"It's complicated." Please, let her leave it there. "I want to hear more about your situation since I really don't have anything to tell you."

"No way. You're not going to get me off topic."

It was time to backpedal a little and find out just how much trouble I would end up in. "Exactly what did my traitorous daughter tell you?" I asked, smiling gratefully at the server who dropped off my chicken Caesar salad, though I wasn't feeling very hungry anymore. This had the potential of going very, very badly.

"She only told me she met your boyfriend, and the three of you went out for burgers last week. I asked her for more details, but she told me to ask you."

Well, she hadn't used his name, which, now that I thought about it, was fairly obvious. The second Rhiannon heard the name, Spencer, she would have been banging down my front door or maybe even kicked it in. "Honestly, she assumed he was my boyfriend, and I sort of think he got a kick out of it."

Rhiannon's eyebrows lifted as she cut into her

grilled chicken. "That's a good sign, right? He didn't run screaming."

"If anything, I think he thought it was funny because he knew it made me uncomfortable." I shrugged when she frowned. "It's hard to explain."

"Who is he? At least tell me what he does for a living. Does he work in the industry?"

"Actually, he's in tech. I don't know the details," I told her, which was the truth. "I wouldn't understand anything about it, anyway."

"A tech bro, huh?" She chuckled, shrugging. "Good for you. I never thought you would be with a guy like that. I always figured you would end up with an actor or at least another lawyer like you."

She was going to find out. She was the only person in my life who knew the name of the man who caused the accident because she was the only one I'd ever told we were dating. As far as Mom and Dad were concerned, I was out with a random man at the time, some Hollywood wannabe I was dating. They thought he ghosted me and ran away to avoid charges, which, on the surface, was exactly what he had done. They thought he left town before I could tell him about the baby, which again was what happened. Just not exactly how I'd explained it in those awful, stressful first days in the hospital. It was better for all of us that they believed my fabrications. The fact that my hospital bills and tuition were covered by the generous settlement went a long way toward them accepting the outcome.

But she knew. And eventually, sooner rather than later, Hannah was going to use his name. Did I want to risk Rhiannon freaking out on her? Maybe even telling her Spencer was her father? Or was it better for me to control the narrative?

When I looked at it that way, there wasn't really a choice to be made.

"I'm going to tell you something." I set down the knife and fork, my heart in my throat, a cold sweat beading on the back of my neck. "But I need you to promise me you won't say a word to Hannah, to Mom and Dad, to anybody."

"Rowan." All the playfulness was gone, replaced by suspicion and maybe a little bit of dread. It wrinkled her forehead and narrowed her eyes. "Who is it? What's the problem?"

Here goes nothing. "A couple of weeks ago, completely by accident, I ran into someone I hadn't seen in a long time." I had to sip my iced tea when my mouth went dry, and that was the only reason I was able to add, "Around eleven years or so."

In many ways, we were as different as sisters

could be. We may have resembled each other, we shared a lot of the same history, and she had my back more times than I would ever be able to count or repay her for, but we had differing temperaments and interests. She had always been patient, and I tended to blow up too quickly.

Those differences were what made it uncanny whenever she was able to see through me the way she clearly did at that table. She lowered her brow, eyes blazing. "No. You are not telling me this."

"Just hang on before you—"

Her silverware clattered onto the plate while horror washed over her face, widening her eyes and making her mouth drop open. "Did you forget what he did? How can this be possible?"

"We aren't seeing each other. That's what I'm trying to tell you."

Blue eyes, much like mine, narrowed in disbelief while her glossy lips tightened in a disapproving line. "No, but you went to dinner with Hannah? You can't be serious!"

By now, a few people around us had noticed her outburst. How could they not? She was practically shrieking. "You need to calm down, please," I begged in a soft voice.

A violent shade of red crept up her neck, then

over her cheeks. "Rowan. He ruined your life. Then he ran away from you. He deserted you."

"That's not technically true."

"Oh, he told you that? Of course he would. He would say anything. And now he knows about Hannah?" She was going to hyperventilate soon if she didn't get a hold of herself.

"Respectfully, you're overreacting."

She clearly didn't care. If anything, she got louder while venom leaked into her voice. "How could you bring him into her life? Are you trying to get her hurt, too, the way you were hurt? What if we can't all support her the way we supported you?"

Her mouth snapped shut, but it was too late. It might have hurt a little less if she had punched me. "Wow," I whispered. "Thanks for that."

She sat back in her chair, shoulders slumped. All the happy, shiny energy was wiped away. "I'm sorry. I didn't mean that the way it came out. I'm worried about you. About Hannah."

"You don't have to worry about me." I picked the napkin up from my lap and dabbed the corners of my mouth before dropping it onto my plate. "As for Hannah, she's my responsibility."

"Come on," she pleaded in a shaky voice. "Don't leave. I only want what's best for you."

"I'm sure you do." I stood, pushing my chair in even when she whimpered. "Which is why you'll be glad to know *we aren't seeing each other*. Like I told you. Please, don't say anything about it. You promised."

As an afterthought before turning away, I added, "I'll Venmo you for my half of the check." It seemed like that hurt her worst of all, making her face crumple. She heaved a sigh behind me, but I ignored her, leaving the restaurant and heading back to the office while a storm raged in my head.

Was she right? Had I lost perspective? The more I thought about it during that seemingly endless walk, the clearer my choice became. I had no business entertaining Spencer's little daydreams about us taking his jet to San Francisco or spending the day at Disneyland. We weren't a family. It was Hannah and me. We were all we needed.

Before I could punk out and betray my daughter —and myself—I texted Spencer from the lobby of my building. This had to be done. It didn't matter how much I didn't want to.

Me: *I think we need to take a step back and reevaluate. We both need a little space.*

This was for the best. I'd thank myself for it later, no matter how I hated myself now.

13

SPENCER

It brought me no pleasure to roll through the tall, ornate iron gates at the entrance to my parents' Malibu estate, where they'd decided to live full time after my father semi-retired. Nothing around here had changed, down to the guard at the gatehouse who lifted a hand in greeting as I passed. I did the same, slowly rolling up the winding driveway leading to the mansion, set far back from the road, away from the eyes of anyone passing by, unlike many other rambling, palatial homes inhabited by the elite of Malibu. Gauche, new money wanted their wealth to be easily viewed from the road. Lawrence Collins, shipping magnate, would never have debased himself that way.

It was a typical, beautiful day. Not a cloud in the

sky, but a storm raged in my head. Some of it was fueled by Rowan's sudden about-face yesterday and the fact that she'd ignored my attempts at reaching out to see what the fuck had changed all of a sudden. Why would she give me the respect of explaining herself? My calls went unanswered, my texts ignored. Was I supposed to hang around, hoping she would come to her senses?

All of that frustration fueled what was already eating a hole through me. I had waited a day after their return, figuring I could do that much not to be accused of bombarding Dad. I had been watching my parents my entire life, and I knew their dynamic. If my mother had the first idea about anything that went down surrounding Rowan, I would have taken the Bentley apart and eaten it piece by piece. I was that sure of myself. It was the old man in my crosshairs this morning.

I left the car in the roundabout, parking beside a marble fountain that shot jets of water into the air that sparkled like diamonds before splashing down. Groundskeepers were hard at work, a few of them nodding in acknowledgment as I charged up the long, wide staircase leading to the front doors.

Rather than wait to be acknowledged, I used my key and strode inside, passing through the marble entry hall and veering right at the grand staircase. The housekeeper exited a room farther down the hall, and her face lit up when she spotted me. A smile tipped the corners of my mouth for the first time all morning. There were times when she was more of a parent to me than either of the people responsible for my birth—exactly the kind of parent I didn't want to be.

"Nora. It's good to see you." Lowering my voice when we were close enough to hear each other, I asked, "How was it having the house quiet for so long?"

She tried and failed to look disapproving. "There was still work to be done to keep things up and running." But it was clear she had enjoyed the break when she winked. "Your mother is with her tennis instructor on the backcourt, and your father is in his study."

Of course he was, and it was precisely why I'd headed in that direction. "I'll surprise him," I told her, patting her shoulder on my way past.

My pleasant expression barely lasted long enough for me to leave her behind. His door was open, sunlight streaming into the hall. My hands tightened into fists as I rounded the doorway without pausing to announce myself.

"Look who it is!" My father said behind a large, oak desk, looking tan and thinner than the last time we saw each other, though it had been months since I'd spent time with him face-to-face. His thick, white hair glowed in the light from the window behind him.

Fuck wasting time. Forget asking how the trip went. Clearly, if he was alive, it went fine. "Congratulations," I announced, striding toward the smug bastard. "You're a grandfather."

It was almost funny, the way his mouth fell open. "What?" he asked with a short, disbelieving laugh.

Coming to a stop in front of him, I said, "*Grandfather*. You have a granddaughter. Congratulations."

He still thought this was a joke, laughing lightly. I could barely stand the sound. "We weren't gone for that long, Spencer."

"You know damn well what I'm talking about."

Lifting his shoulders, he murmured, "I'm sure I don't." The man wasn't human. What little esteem I held him in before today was long gone, thanks to that careless gesture.

"Then allow me to enlighten you." It was gratifying the way his gray eyes widened slightly when I placed my palms on the desk and leaned in. "I have a daughter. She is ten years old. I know you knew

Rowan was pregnant. She told Jarvis. Don't tell me he didn't pass that on."

"Oh. That's what this is about?" Just like that, he collected himself, leaning back in his chair with his hands folded over his flat stomach. "How was I supposed to know she decided to have the child? Don't tell me she looked you up after all this time."

"She never would've done that, and you made sure she wouldn't." I could hardly speak through my gritted teeth, but I managed to add, "I could fucking kill you for this."

His face darkened in time with the narrowing of his eyes. "Remember who you're speaking to."

My back pocket buzzed, but I ignored the call in favor of slamming a fist against the desk hard enough to make his coffee cup rattle. "I know damn well who I'm speaking to, and I would love to rip your head off and shit down your throat for this. How dare you play games like that with other people's lives? That girl was injured, hurting, terrified."

"Yes," he snapped. "And that girl might have decided to press charges while in a heightened emotional state. She could have made life extremely difficult for you. That company of yours?" he asked with a dismissive wave of his hand like it was a joke.

"It wouldn't exist. The people you employ would not have jobs. The comfortable lifestyle you've enjoyed ever since that night? Nothing but a fantasy. I stepped in. I did what a parent does."

"You bullied her. You painted her into a corner. Goddammit," I whispered, getting to the heart of the matter. "You told her to never contact me again. You didn't need to do that. She could have signed an NDA, something vowing to never press charges or go public with the details so long as we paid her bills. But no..." I snarled. "You had to make sure she was out of my life permanently before you ever knew there was a baby, which changed nothing in your eyes."

He stood slowly, unfolding his tall body from the chair and meeting me eye-to-eye. "It's called making tough choices. I thought you knew how that goes. Have you gone soft on me? Is that the problem here?"

"The problem here is, you didn't give either of us a choice."

"She had a choice. She always had one. Nothing was forcing her to sign the document."

"Is that how you sleep at night?" I asked, and the way he scoffed didn't help matters. I could hardly see straight, thanks to the rage blurring my vision while disgust and adrenaline fought for dominance in my system. "Yes, I guess that is the kind of thing you would need to tell yourself. Forget the fact that the girl was in massive pain. She was looking at a future where there was no guarantee she would ever recover. She had just found out she was pregnant. Her career, hopes as an actress were dead, as far as she knew. What did you think she was going to do?"

His mouth opened, but I'd be damned if I listened to another one of his sorry excuses. "I don't need to ask," I snapped, cutting him off. His stunned expression was almost too gratifying. When was the last time anyone spoke to him this way? "You knew what she would do before you sent Jarvis over there. She would look at the dollar sign and all the zeros that came after it, and she would sign because she needed some security after what I did. She needed her hospital bills paid. She needed money to go to school."

My phone rang again, but I ignored it, too intent on him.

"You wonder why I never wanted to work for your fucking company?" Now that I had started, there was no stopping. A flood of sheer hatred poured out of me. I couldn't pretend it didn't feel good to let it go. "All your bullshit about legacy...

keeping it in the family. I learned more about you in the two years I spent in China than in the years I spent living in this house. The way you tend to ignore regulations. The cover-up when it came to incidents caused by negligence, cutting corners where it mattered. I see who you are as a person. All this latest situation did was reinforce what I already knew."

My phone started ringing again, and I might have checked it if it wasn't for the light footsteps coming down the hall. "I swear, this trip ruined my backhand." A second later, Mom rounded the door frame, addressed in tennis whites, with her blonde hair pulled back in a ponytail. It used to come naturally, that hair, but she had started covering her grays as soon as the first one showed up years ago.

"Spencer!" She held her arms out to me, crossing the room, oblivious to the crackling energy filling the room. She was good at that. No doubt it was the only way she was able to remain married to a heartless bastard like him. It wasn't like she needed the money. She had grown up more than comfortable, and her family assets were protected. Was it for status? I was never quite sure.

"You look too thin," I told her after a brief hug

because it was what she loved to hear. "I was having a conversation with Dad."

"A conversation that's now over," my father announced. "I have much too much to take care of now that I'm home. I don't need you coming around, dredging up the past."

"Let me tell you something." Turning away from Mom, I hit him with a glare that sent his ass back into the chair. It was probably for the best that I did not launch myself at him, but I sure as hell wanted to. Good thing for him we now had a witness. "You are the one who's lost out in all of this. You kept them both away from me for ten years, but that's over now."

"What is this all about?" Mom stepped up beside me, placing a hand on my shoulder. "Spencer, what happened?"

I wouldn't have been cruel enough to throw it in her face, but it was clear her own husband didn't care. "Spencer dropped by to inform us we are grandparents," he announced, his voice flat. Mom's sharp gasp was barely audible over the fresh rushing of blood in my ears. This fucking bastard. He would have to bring her into it like that, wouldn't he?

"And you will never see her," I warned as my phone rang yet again and left me wondering what the fuck I was missing. "He will never know her, and he will no longer know me."

"Spencer!" Mom's nails dug into my shoulder. "You don't mean that."

"I mean every word," I told her, glaring at him. His shrewd gaze traveled over my face like he was trying to decide whether I was bluffing. "He will never know the granddaughter he was so callous about. And that's his loss because she's a great kid."

"You know her? You've met her?" The hope in Mom's voice was almost heartbreaking. "I don't understand what any of this is about. Would somebody please tell me?"

Again, my phone rang, and this time, I pulled it from my pocket with a grunt. It was Bruce, who'd called twice now. Vivian had called, as well, along with a few other calls from various managers. I had several missed texts, as well.

"Why don't we all sit down and talk about this?" Mom suggested in a tight voice, high-pitched with worry. "It's so early, Spencer. Have you had breakfast?"

"I have nothing else to say to him." It didn't make me happy, leaving Mom with tears rolling down her cheeks. I knew she had nothing to do with his decisions, but there had to be an emergency to warrant the number of calls and texts I'd ignored, though, which took precedence now. I could smooth things over with her so long as he was never involved.

They let me go without offering any more arguments, and I was on my phone before I reached the staircase opposite the front door. Bruce seemed like the logical person to call first since his call had been the last I received.

As usual, he wasted no time on greetings. "Where the fuck are you? Your assistant told me you've been back and forth between LA and the Bay lately."

"I'm in Malibu. Family shit."

"Well, I hate to break this to you, but you've had a break-in at your company headquarters. Your assistant called me in when she couldn't get a hold of you right away."

I froze halfway down the stairs. The buzzing of bees and chirping of birds went silent. Break-in. Of course, Vivian would call my head of security, Bruce. "What happened? What did they do? Did they take anything? Is everyone all right?"

"It happened early this morning. Before dawn. A coordinated effort, by the looks of it. I'm reviewing the footage with the security team. The front desk guard sustained head injuries."

"Jesus," I whispered, still frozen in place and trying to process the shock. "Do we know how he is?"

"ICU, last I heard."

"What about my offices? What did they take?" I pushed myself forward, jogging to the car. I would be in the air within the hour. This was not something I could handle from afar. I needed to be there, in the middle of it.

"Not much, if anything. Several computers were destroyed. They tried and failed to access the server room. There's a shit ton of broken glass everywhere. The bulk of the damage, I hate to say, was done to your office in particular."

A red flag fluttered in my head by the time I was behind the wheel. "You don't say."

"More than that. A photo was sitting on your chair. No frame. Your assistant told me she'd never seen it before."

"A photo of what?" I asked, already eager to get the call over with so I could call my pilot.

"I'm not sure. You're in it, along with a blonde woman and a little blonde girl. Walking out of a restaurant together."

Halfway to the gates, I slammed the brakes and screeched to a halt. Everything in me wanted to reject the image Bruce was putting together. Somebody was sending a message, something about how easy it was to get to me. And the people I cared about. Nausea gripped my stomach, but I couldn't give in. There was no time.

All at once, the world took on a newfound clarity. My priorities aligned, and I hit the gas again, tearing down the driveway now. "I'm going to call you back in fifteen minutes," I told Bruce. "There are things I'm going to need from your contacts down here, so get a list together. Security, mostly."

If there was one thing I appreciated about him, it was the way he didn't need to ask questions. "Will do."

I would kill the son of a bitch for this. He couldn't get Miles and decided to turn his attention to me instead. It was the biggest and last mistake Damian Fields would ever make. First on my list was placing a call to someone who might be able to help.

Every breath through my tightened throat was a chore, and my heart was ready to crack open my chest, hammering the way it was. Somehow, I placed a call to my cousin, Connor, somebody with the resources to help, thanks to his media empire. I normally wouldn't have fallen back on family ties, but this was not a normal situation.

I waited a few moments to be connected before Connor's rich, hearty voice filled the car. Mom was his father's baby sister, one of those late-in-life second-family situations, meaning she and her nephew were roughly the same age. In some ways, he was more of a father to me than my own, someone I'd looked up to as a kid. "Spencer! This is a pleasant surprise. What can I do for you?"

Time to cut to the chase. "Remember what I told you about Damian Fields back in the Hamptons?"

"Are you kidding? My digital division has been hell-bent on turning Miles into a hero online. What's going on now?"

I gave him a brief rundown while navigating traffic. It was getting thicker all the time, slowing me down and making it difficult not to scream. I had to get back to Rowan and Hannah. What if that photo was more than a warning?

"I see." Connor's voice turned hard, with a thread of cold ruthlessness running underneath. "What do you need me to do?"

"I need you to syndicate a story for me once I've located the witnesses in question. If you can help me track them down, I'd appreciate it. I've got a guy working for me out here, but he's come up with nothing." And we were running out of time. A man with Connor's resources and influence would make all of this much easier to manage.

"Whatever you want, you've got it," he vowed. "Just tell me who they are. I can have a couple of private eyes on it by lunch." Considering he was three hours ahead of me and his lunch would roll around within the hour, that was quite a promise.

It was time to take the fight to the next level since Damian wouldn't give up unless I forced him.

He was going to wish he had never started this.

14

———

ROWAN

"Rowan? I have Lex Landry's office for you."

My head snapped up at Noelle's announcement through my desk phone's speaker. All I wanted was a quiet Friday after a hellaciously busy week and a night of broken sleep after the fight with Rhiannon and a text to Spencer which I knew must have hurt him. If only I didn't care so much whether I hurt him.

Now, I had an unexpected call from a studio boss. Why would he call directly? It didn't matter that I tried to tell myself there was nothing wrong. My stomach churned in the second it took to lift the phone receiver and tap the blinking button to the extension where Lex waited. "Mr. Landry. What can I do for you?"

"So that's what it takes to get your attention?" Spencer's voice held a sharp, bitter sort of humor. "I have to pretend to be somebody you feel like talking to?"

Son of a bitch. After his several attempts to reach out yesterday afternoon, I blocked him for the rest of the day. Clearly, we had different ideas about what it meant when a person requested space. It was never my intention to block him permanently. At least, not until now. "Not cool. You're wasting my time now. I wasn't kidding when I said I need space."

"Listen to me. This isn't about that." After that came a shout. "Stupid fuck! Get off the road!"

"Excuse me?"

"I'm in the car," he grunted out. "Traffic out of Malibu is a fucking nightmare. Something very big has come up. Very important. I need you to follow directions and not ask any questions. I'll answer them later."

"Uh, *sure.*" I had to laugh off my discomfort. Noelle and I would need to have a talk about properly vetting my phone calls. "I'll get right on that for you."

"Rowan," he barked loudly enough to make my

head snap back. "This is serious. I need you to get Hannah out of school and take her to the Beverly Wilshire. I'm probably being overcautious, but I don't want to take unnecessary risks."

Dread slithered up my spine, but I tried to ignore it. "You want me to do what? Why? You're out of your mind."

"*Please,* Rowan. Listen to me. I know it's a lot to ask but there's a good reason for it. I'll explain when I get there." A car horn blared in the background.

"You can't call me and order me around like this. As if I can drop everything at a moment's notice, all because you said so." Was this his way of forcing us into the same room? Ignoring my needs? Rhiannon was right. I shouldn't have brought him into our lives.

"Please, get mad at me later. Right now, I need you to get Hannah and get to the damn hotel. Don't tell anybody where you're going, and don't stop at home for anything. We'll figure that out."

The dread was starting to spread, lighting up the darkest corners of my brain. This wasn't a joke. No way he'd keep up the act for this long.

"I made the reservation in Lex's name," he continued. "There's a standing order to keep a suite free for any big shots he wants to impress. I let the staff know you're on your way. Use Lex's name, not your own. Do you understand? That is critical."

Suddenly, I was very scared. "I don't understand any of this," I whispered over the fear rising in my chest.

"I know. I'll explain when I get there. Do as I say... *please.*"

"All right." He had me freaked out, to say the least. Were we in danger? How could we be? How long were we supposed to stay at the hotel? He had a hell of a lot of explaining to do.

In the meantime, I had to explain this to my daughter when I didn't have the first idea what was going on. It was a good thing in retrospect that I'd been so busy earlier in the week, meaning fewer meetings scheduled for today.

After doing a little last-minute rescheduling with Noelle, I headed out under the pretext of an emergency, which might not have been a lie.

"WHY ARE WE DOING THIS?" Hannah's wide eyes sparkled with mischief as we walked to the car after I pulled her out of school for the day. It wasn't something I'd ever done, meaning this was a big adventure for her. "Where are we going?"

Only a mother would understand what it meant to pretend everything was fine when inside, the opposite was true. "We're going to have a special weekend. It's going to be a big adventure. Spencer got us a penthouse suite at the Beverly Wilshire as a surprise, and I thought it would be fun to get there early." What a lame excuse.

Good thing she was a very excited ten-year-old who wasn't currently in the mood to think logically. "Really? Cool!"

"So you're excited?"

"Mom!" I remembered being her age, unable to believe my parents didn't get it. "Do you know how many famous people stay there all the time? There's always pictures of people walking in and out of there. Maybe we'll see somebody!"

"Wouldn't that be neat?" Because yes, let her be excited. Let her focus on that and not on how strange all of this was. She could afford to be happy while I wrestled with a hundred questions, each worse than the last. What could possibly have happened?

The check-in process was seamless. Certain

names earned respect in this town, and Lex's was one of them. Hannah was too enamored of our surroundings to notice the name I gave, looking around the lobby like she was hoping to spot a celebrity. By the time we headed for the elevator, she was bouncing on the balls of her feet. "This is so cool. Everybody at school is going so jealous when I tell them."

Instinctively, I knew this was a bad idea. "I don't think you should do that," I told her on our way up to the suite. When she shot me a confused look, I explained, "This is a secret adventure. What happens if they find out at school that I pulled you out to take you to a hotel to have fun? No, this is going to have to be our secret. But secrets can be fun, right?"

"Yeah. I guess so." It seemed like I had popped her balloon.

Her disappointment didn't last long. All it took was opening the door onto a spacious, gorgeous suite to leave her squealing. "There's a piano! Right in the living room!" She ran to it, then turned to me. "Do you remember how to play?"

"I haven't played in years," I told her, and I was a little disappointed. It wasn't like I had a lot of opportunities to practice as the years went on. Life had sort of gotten in the way.

There was so much more to admire—the spa-like bathroom and the king beds in both large, sunny bedrooms. "King-size! It's huge!" I knew before my daughter finished kicking off her shoes what she was about to do.

"Please, be careful," I begged, but there was laughter in my voice as she climbed onto the bed and started jumping. At least one of us was happy.

The lock on the door buzzed, signaling someone was using the keypad to enter. I left Hannah to her jumping and strode out to the living room, where Spencer just about launched himself through the door with his head on a swivel, looking for us.

When his gaze landed on me, it softened. "You're safe. Thank God." He reached for me, touching my cheek and taking my hand in his. Dammit, why did he have to touch me that way? I needed space. I needed time. I needed to make sense of the past and decide how much of a place it deserved in the present.

All of that flew out the window the second his skin touched mine.

I held a finger to my lips, looking down the hall to where Hannah was still bouncing her heart out. "We're having a big adventure," I told him.

I motioned for him to follow me onto the terrace,

where small sofas and chairs were clustered together so people could sit and admire the view of Rodeo Drive. It was stunning and would be even more so once night fell and everything lit up.

At the moment, I couldn't have cared less. "What is going on?" I whispered, leaving the glass door open a crack so I would hear if Hannah called out.

He looked like a man who had been through the wringer. His hair was a mess, as if his fingers had raked through it endlessly. His eyes were bleary. There were sweat stains under his arms when he stretched, his hands around the railing, bending at the waist and staring at the tile under our feet. "This is all my fault. I didn't tell you everything, and I lost sight of the big picture."

I knew it. I knew there had to be a catch. When would I ever learn to listen to my instincts? No, I had to go and ignore them, making excuses, telling myself it was better for me to control the narrative and bring him into our lives.

Leopards didn't change their spots. He was never going to be completely honest with me unless there was a catastrophe and someone forced his hand. It seemed like we had reached that stage.

"Are you going to tell me what it's about?" I asked. "Do I get to know why it was so important I take my daughter out of school early today and check into this hotel under a different name?"

"Please." He held up a hand, still not looking at me. "You have no idea what's been going through my head the past two hours. I have to catch my breath and think."

"You had better do it in a hurry, or else I'm taking her out of here—"

His head snapped up, eyes blazing, jaw clenched. "No. Not until I know for sure it's safe for you to do that."

"Why would it not be safe? What have you gotten us into?"

First, he blew out a deep breath. "You remember when we first went out, and I told you there was somebody looking to undercut me and my business partner?"

"You mean when all you wanted was to make sure I wouldn't spill my guts?" I rolled my eyes. "Yeah. I remember that."

"That piece of shit has also committed arson against his opponents prior to this."

The late morning sun was warm, but it did nothing for the sudden icy cold that washed over me. "He what?"

"Not that we've ever been able to confirm it was

him," he continued. "But it's a pattern. Before dawn this morning, my headquarters were vandalized. My office was torn to pieces."

How did that tie into anything? It sucked, certainly. "That's awful. I'm sorry."

He swallowed hard, going pale. "Whoever did it left behind a photo of the three of us. From the sound of it, the photo was taken while we were leaving dinner last week."

Finally, we were at the heart of the matter. He had taken the long way around, but now we were seeing eye to eye.

And there was one second, no more than that, when I saw myself pitching him over the railing and letting him fall after putting my baby in harm's way. Now I understood the urgency. The secrecy. The fact that we had to go straight to the hotel without even stopping off for clothes.

A shockwave rolled over me, making me grip the railing to hold myself upright. "What you're telling me is…" I whispered, shaking. "Hannah and I could've been in danger because of you. And that if you had left us alone, we wouldn't be in danger. Does that about sum it up?"

"He might have found you either way." Just when I

was about to scream, he added, "But yes, I sped up the process. I know that. I should have known he would get desperate once we squashed all the shit he dug up on Miles." He raked a hand through his hair, groaning.

"You knew this man was dangerous, and you neglected to add that part when you told me about him?"

"I didn't think—"

"That's right! You didn't think! You pulled our daughter into this, and you didn't fucking think about it! How could you be so oblivious?"

I wanted him to fight. To shout and defend himself. I wanted an excuse to tear into him. What he gave me was a resigned sigh and slumped shoulders. "You're absolutely right. I lost sight of what mattered."

"That's a nice way of saying you dropped the fucking ball," I muttered.

"You think this isn't killing me? Do you think my stomach didn't drop when I heard about that photo?"

"Poor you," I retorted, shaking my head and looking him up and down. It was like I had never seen him before. Just when I thought I understood him. "It's killing you? I have a child in there who depends on me, and you put her in danger. Sorry if I don't pity you."

He straightened slowly, his features twisting in disappointment when he looked down at me. "She's my daughter too. You don't think I'm afraid for her? You don't think she was my first thought?"

My heart swelled despite me very much wanting it not to. I needed it to harden, not to melt over a few empty words. "How would I know?" I countered. "You can decide at any point that you would rather walk away."

He threw his arms into the air, barking out a laugh. "What do I have to do to prove I'm not interested in walking away? I don't do that unless I'm forced into it by asshole parents, or have you forgotten?"

When he reached for me, I backed away, refusing to be touched. No matter how much I wanted to be in his arms and rest my aching head against his chest. This was all so much, and I needed something to cling to.

But this was also his fault. "What do we do?" I asked, wrapping my arms around my trembling body. "How am I supposed to give her a life if we have to worry about this guy following us, maybe hurting us?"

"I swear to you, I'm working on that. This is going to end soon." He lowered his brow, nostrils flaring, teeth grinding. It was both chilling and strangely exciting. "He's going to regret ever drawing his first breath by the time I'm finished with him. The point of getting you two here was making sure you're safe while we figure out what comes next. I'm going to arrange for security in the meantime."

His hands cupped my shoulders, and this time, I couldn't fight him off. Not when I needed his nearness more than anything. Something real, solid, strong. For too long, I'd had to rely on myself and my family for Hannah's needs. But what about me? For once, I just needed the physical support, the comfort for me. And here he was, offering me what I so desperately wanted. And as I let my body take what he was offering, my mind drifted back to how we got here, the frantic phone call. It was enough to know he was in this. That he cared.

I let him pull me in and wrap his arms around me tightly enough to squeeze the air from my lungs. His heart pounded wildly under my ear when I touched it to his firm chest. The throbbing in my head eased like magic. We would get through this. How did the impossible seem possible now that I was with him?

"I've got this. I've got *you*." His lips pressed against my forehead, then my temple, turning the iciness in my veins to something warmer and very familiar. Maybe it was so many days spent without his touch, his kiss. Maybe it was the heightened emotion and excitement of the day.

Whatever it was, it convinced me to tilt my head back and be kissed by him. To let him sweep me away with his lips, with his soft, urgent breaths. With his tongue, once it stroked mine, delving into my mouth, claiming it the way he had so many times before. I would never get tired of it.

What was happening to me? This was the man I should've resented to my last breath. Instead, I was clinging to him, kissing him hard, searching for some connection in the middle of so much confusion. He buried a hand in my hair, his touch tender and passionate. My pussy warmed and went moist as deep desire flared to life. Pleasure replaced fear, promising escape. Oblivion. I craved it with all of me.

There was one problem.

"I'm walking into the living room now!" Hannah's voice rang out, echoing in the suite thanks to the way she raised it. "So if any grown-ups are kissing, they should stop!"

She must have already come out and spotted us. We laughed together before I ran my hands over my hair, putting it back into place. "Good thing nobody's doing that!" I called out, extricating myself from Spencer's embrace and opening the door further. It was time to put on a happy face again. "I have an idea. Let's order room service. I skipped breakfast, and I'm starved."

Hannah and Spencer exchanged a glance that contained a thousand words. "Do they have ice cream on the menu?" she asked.

For once, I wouldn't put up an argument. Not this weekend.

15

SPENCER

Throughout the day, I'd started forcing myself to push it to the back of my mind for Hannah's sake, but over the course of the afternoon and evening, I had been able to forget about it once in a while, even as Hannah went on an endless monologue about her favorite pop singers. Wasn't she too young for that? I didn't know shit about it, apparently.

Roughly twelve hours after I learned about the break-in, Bruce finally had a report for me. When the call came through, I stepped into one of the two bedrooms and closed the door while Rowan and Hannah played around on the piano in the living room. The sounds of their laughter mingled with the tinkling of the keys. Somehow that made the reason for the call seem that much darker in comparison.

"The good news is, nothing was permanently damaged," he shared. "The few machines they broke are easily replaceable, and everything on them was backed up to the shared server. It doesn't look like they were able to access anything, either," he added.

My chest tightened, and a telltale pounding in my head left me closing my eyes and forcing a few slow breaths. "But they *did* try to access files?" I asked.

"It looks that way. Whoever was behind this was a real fucking amateur," he concluded with a wry chuckle. "The whole thing looks a lot like a way to throw us off."

"To make it look like hacking the machines was the goal," I mused, and he grunted his agreement.

"As for security," he continued. "Everything is set. I have a pair of cars working in shifts on the McNultys' block, and I have another pair of cars with eyes on that apartment building your girl lives in."

She's not my girl. My silent, knee-jerk response brought with it a sense of disappointment. Did I want her to be? My gut said yes, but she was still so damn skittish over Hannah, making sure not to let her down if things didn't work out between us. I had to find a way to convince her there was nothing to worry about.

Bruce didn't need to know that, and there wasn't time. "I want somebody watching Hannah's school until this is over too." Her high-pitched giggles made my chest tighten again, though in a different way. If anything ever happened to her...

"I can arrange that," he assured me. "I was in touch with your cousin, Mr. Diamond. I have to say, the private investigator he hired is thorough."

Was there a little resentment in his voice? Or was it the sound of one professional begrudgingly complimenting another? "Does that mean you have good news?" I asked.

"It means we're making headway. Those bastards can run, but they can't hide. I hope to have more specifics for you in the morning, though I'll call if anything major comes up between now and then."

"Good enough. Talk then." I ended the call, releasing a long, slow breath. We were making head-way. The pair of backstabbing assholes who broke ranks and went to work for Damian couldn't hide forever. Connor's investigator would find them, and we would put an end to this for good.

Then what?

Rowan finished the song she had slowly played

her way through, laughing loud enough for the sound to reach me and stir my heart. "I told you I'm awful at this!" she squealed while Hannah laughed harder than she had all day.

Was this what it meant to be a parent? I kept swinging between wanting to know everything about her and coming up with reasons to worry about her. Would she be safe at school? The idea of somebody watching her, following her home, sent adrenaline racing through my veins.

Rowan and I had a lot of talking to do. For now, I shook it off, opening the bedroom door. "So, now we know why your mom chose law over becoming a pianist," I told Hannah, who blurted out a laugh while Rowan flipped me off from behind her, smirking.

THE SOFT KNOCK on my bedroom door was expected. No. I had waited for it, lying in bed, flipping through channels on the television and knowing Rowan would join me once she knew Hannah was asleep. The meaningful looks we'd exchanged while the two of them were on their way to the second bedroom told an entire story.

"Come in," I murmured, sitting up with my back to the headboard. It had taken longer than I'd expected for her to sneak out of their room, to the point where I'd given up on sharing a drink and gotten dressed for bed instead. It made sense when I thought about it. The kid was amped up after an exciting day and going to bed in new surroundings. Naturally, it took a little time for her to wind down.

Rowan crept in, wearing one of the two matching nightshirts I'd ordered up to the suite earlier. Hannah had loved the idea of wearing pajamas that matched her mom's. "She would not settle in," she whispered, closing the door softly. "I shouldn't stay for long in case she wakes up."

My breath caught as I watched her cross the room. There was no end to my desire for her. My gaze was immediately drawn to her tits, gently swaying under the striped satin. She climbed onto the bed, sitting cross-legged, facing me to ask, "How long do we need to do this?"

"If I had my way, we'd stay here until everything is settled."

"What does that mean, though?" She tucked her hair behind both ears, suddenly looking very young and worried. "What is settled?"

There was no resisting those smooth, sleek legs,

only inches from me. I reached over and ran a hand over her calf, savoring her silky skin. "Once I know Damian is taken care of, and no, I don't know exactly how long that will be. In the meantime, I'll have security working in shifts at your apartment building, Hannah's school, your parents' house. Your office building, too, if you want," I added as an afterthought while she gaped at me.

"What?" Her mouth dropped open. "You're kidding."

"I'm not taking any chances. They'll be discreet," I insisted. "I can't let her go to school unprotected every day when that bastard knows who she is. You can't ask me to do that."

"I don't understand why this has to happen." Her head hung, swinging back and forth while she took a hitching breath. "It's all too much."

"I'm going to take care of it. This is all going to end, and it's going to end well for you and Hannah." Covering her hand with mine, I added, "You have my word. Nobody is going to hurt you."

"I don't know what to tell Mom and Dad. They deserve to know." Her lips pulled together in a thin line. "I've never told them anything about you. Us. They still think you were some random guy I dated for a little while before you ghosted me."

"After I almost killed you." My gaze drifted to the scars I had already started to overlook. They were part of her, but only a small part. I slid closer, reaching out and stroking her hair, taking the chance of letting my fingers trace those thin lines. It could have meant taking my life in my hands, but she didn't stop me, going still and holding her breath while I studied the wreckage I had caused. "I am so sorry," I whispered. "I didn't get the chance to tell you then... while you were conscious, anyway," I added.

"Not that I'm trying to let you off the hook," she murmured, meeting my gaze with those frank, blue eyes. "But I meant it when I told you I'm doing fine. Life turned out the way it was supposed to."

I wasn't sure I agreed. Not for myself. Professionally, life couldn't be better, but there was so much more to life than business. I had missed the first ten years of my daughter's life. How was that preferable to being with her?

There were no answers. Trying to find them was a waste of time, especially when there were better things to do , like cupping the back of her head in my hand and pulling her in, leaning close to brush my lips over hers. A sizzle ran through me, making my dick jump in anticipation.

"I can't stay," she whispered as I took her mouth again, this time teasing her with my tongue, stroking hers until she let out one of her helpless, throaty moans, which never failed to stoke the fire already starting to burn.

I was acutely aware that Hannah could walk in at any moment, yet the thrill of the risk only intensified my desire, making each kiss feel like a reckless gamble.

She shifted her weight until she was lying on her side. I followed her down, facing her, pulling her body close while undoing her one kiss at a time. My hand slid over the satin nightshirt and the luscious curves underneath it, my heart pounding, my hunger growing with every caress. When she draped a leg over my hip, pulling me in, that hunger exploded.

I growled, grabbing her ass and tugging her closer, grinding my insistent erection against her pussy. My mouth ran over her throat while her fingers danced through my hair, and she panted in my ear. "Spencer... oh God... I should go... let me go."

"Go?" I grunted, running my tongue across her clavicle. "Tell me what you *really* want." I peppered soft kisses down her neck, lingering at the sensitive spot just above her collarbone. Every moan that escaped her lips signaled her surrender, her struggle fading as a desperate hunger took its place, mirroring my own.

"Tell me..." I insisted, my voice low and urgent.

"I want you inside me," she breathed out as she quickly reached between us, cupping me, her fingers dipping inside the waistband of my boxer briefs and freeing my aching dick. I growled against her skin, losing control for a second and moving against her, straining, fighting for the friction I so desperately needed.

Before this could go further, I rolled away from her, fumbling through the nightstand for a condom while she sat up and pulled the nightshirt over her head. I was frozen stiff at the sight of those gorgeous tits falling free, then forgot about the condom in favor of tasting her pert nipples, attacking them like I was starved. Her nails scraped the back of my neck, my shoulders, setting my skin on fire, making me suck harder, teasing her with my tongue and teeth until she bit back a high-pitched cry.

"Lie back," she whispered, hands on my shoulders. I was too surprised to resist, watching her push up onto her knees and then lift my hips when she started to lower my underwear.

Fuck me. Yes. She treated me to her mouth first, taking me in all at once. My head dropped back onto the pillow, my senses overloaded thanks to the sheer pleasure of her warm mouth, her firm tongue against my underside. "Fuuuck... just like that," I begged, moving my hips, giving her more. She gagged slightly when I hit the back of her throat, but she adjusted, always eager to take as much of me as possible. I never did meet another woman who loved giving head the way she did.

Pressure built in my balls and promised relief while wet slurping sounds blended with my quick pants for air. I was tempted to chase that high but instead eased her off me, reaching for the foil pack again. She helped me, rolling the latex down my length, surprising me for the second time.

I laid back, hands behind my head, and watched as she lowered her panties. There wasn't a doubt in my mind she would be dripping wet by now.

She straddled me and took me in hand, then ran my head through those juices until it glistened. Her face contorted in pleasure as she guided me inside her, making me clench my teeth as her tight sheath enveloped me.

"So damn tight, baby," I grunted out, almost overwhelmed.

"Fuck, yes," she agreed, lowering herself to my base with her eyes closed. She stayed there for a moment or two, breathing hard, before she started to move, slowly grinding her clit against me, taking me deep.

"Look at me," I whispered. Her eyes opened and met mine, held my gaze as she rose and fell. I watched desire flare in them, watched them go hazy and unfocused in time with her muscles gripping me tighter. I reached out and took her hips in my hands, fingers pressing into her creamy flesh as I jerked her down harder, thrusting upward as I did.

"Oh... mmm, Spencer... yes, f-fuck me..." Her hands landed on my chest, and she leaned on them, working hard, riding me until a rhythmic clapping filled the room in time with our bodies crashing together.

And when she came, it was with a strangled cry, one hand over her mouth, as she collapsed on top of me. Her muscles quivered, milking me, promising release. I let go gladly and pressed my fist to my mouth, barely holding back the groan stirring in my throat while my balls emptied.

How the hell had I gone so long without this? Without the magic of her? Everything was more intense—deeper, stronger. And when it came time for her to roll away with a weak sigh, there was a touch of regret that went along with it. Like I was losing her again.

I needed to be careful, or I might end up going too far and asking if she could see us doing this for the rest of our lives. It had to be the aftermath of coming, mixed with the fact that our daughter was sleeping in the next room.

That had to be why this felt so right.

I mulled it over long after Rowan slipped out of the room, wanting to be there if Hannah woke up.

I mulled over a lot of things once I was alone again.

16

ROWAN

"Do you guys have any questions for me? Are you okay with all of this?"

My parents exchanged the sort of look they had perfected during the course of their marriage. Somehow, they were able to hold a full conversation without saying a word. Dad's trademark skeptical frown was on full display when he turned my way on the familiar old couch where I used to change Hannah's diapers.

Every corner of this house held a memory.

"I don't know how I feel about this," he admitted, gruff but gentle as always. "All this time, you told us one story, and now we hear a totally different story?"

"Charles." Mom shook her head gently, leaning over to give my hand a reassuring pat. "Let's not get ahead of ourselves. We both knew there was more to the story than Rowan was letting on. There's no need to pretend."

When I shot a look of pure surprise her way, she continued, "Come on. You told us you were dating some Hollywood nobody, yet that same nobody could afford a sports car, which we never saw because the accident was cleared up and all evidence was erased. This is someone who had the means to not only pay for your medical bills but to cover your tuition. Obviously, this was not a random nobody off the street."

"We didn't want to press you on it," Dad continued, sounding almost relieved now that there was no need to pretend. "You had already been through so much, and we all knew you had a long road ahead of you. Not only with your injuries but with the baby on the way. It seemed kinder and healthier to let you move on in any way you could."

What did I expect? They weren't stupid. I should have known they had their suspicions, but it had been easier at the time to imagine I'd told a decent lie.

"All right, that's settled," I concluded, a little shaken and maybe slightly embarrassed. I honestly thought they'd bought it. "But how do you feel about needing security, just in case?"

"It doesn't make me feel good," Dad admitted, rubbing a hand over his neatly trimmed gray beard. "I would much rather take Hannah somewhere safe if that's the concern."

"I don't know if that would help," I admitted. "Granted, I don't know much about any of this. He swears this is all going to blow over soon, and he's only acting out of an overabundance of caution. He is deeply invested in Hannah's welfare."

"Convenient, so many years later," Dad grumbled while Mom clicked her tongue at him.

"It's complicated," I murmured. For the sake of wrapping this up sometime tonight, I left out a lot of key details. They only knew Hannah's father was a wealthy man from a wealthy family whose father had arranged for everything to be silenced. They didn't know about the details of the document I signed or any specifics. I hadn't even told them his last name. The less they knew, the better until we came up with a plan to move forward.

If I wanted to move forward.

The truth was, when I checked in with my heart, there was nothing I wanted more except for Hannah's happiness and safety, of course. But it seemed like Spencer played a big role in that, at least when it came to happiness. They got along famously, like two peas in a pod.

I couldn't pretend my mama heart didn't swell when I saw them together. He was the missing piece of our puzzle. All I had to do was let down my guard and allow things to progress.

For both of them and us.

"You know I'm going to check on you ten times a day," Spencer had told me as we parted ways at the hotel earlier that Sunday afternoon. Our body-guards were in place. What a bizarre thought, but then Spencer had pointed out the fact that children of wealthy families often had a bodyguard around them. *"I don't want my daughter out there in the world unprotected,"* he had insisted.

On one hand, it was sweet to know how invested he was in her well-being. On the other? I didn't love the idea of my daughter belonging in a world where she needed protection. There was still part of me that wasn't ready to accept this.

"Just ignore the guys sitting outside. You both will be safe," I made sure to remind my parents. "But don't be surprised if I check in with you a bunch of times." I was starting to sound like Spencer.

I left them to process what I had just dropped on

their heads, going upstairs to visit with Hannah before I left. She was lying diagonally across the bed on her stomach, her feet swinging back and forth in the air while she read a book. The sight of her being so carefree made my heart ache in a good way. If only I could keep her this innocent forever, this untouched by the world.

"I'm going to head out, kiddo," I told her. "But I'll be here Friday, same as always. And I'll give you a call tonight, before bed," I added, eyeing the flip phone Spencer had given Hannah earlier. It couldn't hurt being able to get in touch with her, and it was—in her words—a dumb phone. It only made calls and sent texts.

"*Back in my day, we just called a phone,*" Spencer had remarked with a wry grin. "*This is in case you ever need to get in touch with me or with your mom. For any reason, even if you just want to talk. Our numbers are already in there.*" She had accepted the device happily enough, though I sensed her disappointment at it not being a smartphone.

"And can I call you anytime I want to?" she asked. I nodded, sitting beside her on the bed and kissing the top of her head. She rolled onto her back, looking up at me, her forehead creased like she had something on her mind. I waited, giving her space instead of forcing her to vocalize whatever was on her mind.

"Can I ask you something?" she whispered.

"Of course."

"Is Spencer my dad?"

I knew it was coming. This was a smart little girl, insightful, somebody who never missed a beat. If anything, I might have been worried if she hadn't put two and two together by the time our weekend at the Beverly Wilshire was over. He was so interested in her, almost voracious. He wanted to make up for all the time he had lost.

She wasn't letting me off the hook, those expressive blue eyes studying me as I fumbled around, trying to come up with the right thing to say. Finally, I asked, "What makes you ask that question?"

"Mom. I'm not a baby. He's, like, the only man you ever introduced me to. And there was that one time when we were having dinner last night when he was talking about something you guys did together a long time ago. Then there's the same eyes and shaped face we share."

Dammit. I knew she would pick up on that when Spencer had asked if I remembered a trip we took to San Francisco one night. He'd flown me there in the family jet to show off a little. He had laughed about how ordinary the trip was for him a decade later, how he had never expected at the time to build a business up there. He'd never expected to build a business in the first place. The Spencer I used to know had no ambitions.

I wouldn't insult her by coming up with a well-intended lie. Instead, I gave her the sort of straightforward answer she always appreciated. "Yes. Spencer is your dad, honey." There it was. No taking it back. After giving her a minute to process, I asked, "How do you feel about it?"

"I like him." The fact that she didn't hesitate was a good sign. "He's nice. He's fun. He listens. And you like him."

"Now, wait a second." She wasn't wrong, but it would be a mistake not to set her straight for both our sakes. "I'm not actually dating Spencer. It's complicated. Yes, we do like each other, but that doesn't mean we're going to, you know..." Oh, this was pathetic. I should have practiced a speech in advance.

"It doesn't mean you're going to get married or anything?" she concluded.

"Exactly." She frowned, and I was sorry I couldn't give her the answer she wanted. The answer *I* wanted. "But one thing I'm sure about is how crazy he is about you. He wants to spoil you rotten. He thinks you're amazing, just like I do. You're a lucky little girl to have so many people who adore you."

"I know lots of kids whose parents aren't married," she reasoned, but I heard the disappointment in her voice. My chest went tight at the sound of it. Well, life wasn't always cut and dry. There were complications. She was going to learn that sooner or later, right? I certainly had. Not that it made me feel better for her.

"We'll make it work," I promised. "But just between you and me, let's pretend we didn't have this talk. Spencer might want to tell you himself, in his own way."

"Don't worry." A playful grin tipped the corners of her mouth. "I'll act like I don't know."

"Thank you, sweetheart. I love you." I gathered her in my arms and held her close, closing my eyes and breathing her in. Nobody was going to hurt her. I had to believe that, or else I would never be able to let go.

But I did with another promise to call her before bed. I had a ton of work to catch up on after spending the weekend pretty much offline. It was disappointing the circumstances were what they were because otherwise, I might have looked back on the weekend as a mini vacation. I didn't know many vacations that involved essentially being locked in a hotel suite, having meals delivered, and having clothes and toiletries brought up.

To Hannah, it had been a huge adventure, a splurge. If only she could remain that innocent.

"Too bad it's late spring."

Noelle's random comment made me look up from my MacBook in surprise. "What was that?" I asked with a laugh.

She touched a finger to the lush bouquet of red roses on my desk and turned slightly, motioning toward the pink and white bouquets on my credenza. Three in total, delivered every morning this week. "I was thinking we could have entered your office in the Tournament of Roses Parade, that was back in January."

"You should be a comedian, you know that?" I struggled to hide my grin.

"So, who is this guy with all the extra cash to send you two dozen roses a day?"

Okay, so maybe he was going a little over the top, but I couldn't pretend I disapproved. I had gone a decade without him, without any steady man in my life. There was a lot of spoiling to be made up for. "He's an old friend," I told her, clocking her skeptical expression and ignoring it.

"An old friend who's been texting you all day, every day? Come on," she continued with a laugh when I sputtered, trying to come up with an excuse. "I see the look on your face when you get a text from him."

"Exactly what kind of look is that?" I asked, tipping my chair back and arching an eyebrow.

She should have been an actress. All at once, her cheeks went pink while she sank her teeth into her bottom lip, barely biting back a smile. Her eyes twinkled, and she let out a tiny giggle.

"I don't giggle like that," I deadpanned.

"But you do make that face," she insisted, grinning. "This isn't just an old friend. An old friend doesn't spend hundreds of bucks like it's nothing."

As if on cue, my phone buzzed, sitting face down on the desk. It was like something out of an old Western movie showdown. I stared at her. She stared at me. Would I pick up the phone, or would I ignore it? Would I react exactly the way she described?

"Check it already," she finally groaned out. "I know you're dying to."

"It can wait," I decided. Yes, I wanted to answer the damn thing, but I couldn't forget all of my responsibilities in favor of fawning over my crush. I wasn't in high school anymore.

We finished going over my schedule for the following day, and she sauntered out of my office. "Now you can check your phone in peace," she teased, disappearing. Her soft laughter faded to silence as I turned the phone over to read the latest message.

Spencer: *Thinking about flying down tonight. Do you know anybody who might be in the mood for dinner? Around 8:00 or so?*

Did I? The way my heart jumped into my throat, there was no question about it. I was wondering if we would see each other during the week or if we'd have to wait until the weekend, but I didn't want to ask. My pride wouldn't let me, and it felt like I would be needy to ask for more of him than he was ready to give.

This would have been complicated enough without Hannah being involved, but I had to think of her first and foremost. I couldn't bring anyone into her life unless I was sure they'd be there permanently. It was one thing for her to know Spencer was her father, but another for us to play house like there was a future for us. It wouldn't only be my heart that ended up breaking.

We'll talk about it tonight. Yes, that felt right. It was time to start thinking about the next steps after Damian was no longer a problem. Because as long as I was being honest with myself, I wanted more of him than the occasional weeknight fling or a weekend with Hannah. I wanted him just as much as I ever had, if not more.

Back in the day, I had wanted the Spencer I used to know. Now, I also wanted the rest of him. The man he had become. I only needed to be sure he wanted me. Or else I was setting myself up for another broken heart.

And this time, there wouldn't be any coming back from it.

Me: *I'll ask around, but I'm sure I can find somebody who would be interested.*

I bit my lip, grinning, when I imagined him reading that and growling. Shit, I fell hard, didn't I?

The fact was, there was part of me that had never stopped loving him despite everything. I hadn't fully understood that until now.

17

———

SPENCER

"Mmm... yes. Just like that."

I craved the sound of her moans. On the touch of her hands on the back of my head, holding me in place, fighting for release. The way she humped my face, grinding, breathing faster, all the while her juices coated my tongue. It only made me want more, and I was greedy enough to drive my tongue deep inside her, as far as I could go, to taste every last drop.

"Shi-it, yesss!" Her hips lifted, jerking, her legs spreading wider. "Holy fuck, that's so good!"

It was, and I didn't think I'd ever have enough.

Opening my eyes, I gazed across her writhing body, watching her tits rise and fall with every sharp breath as her orgasm built. She cupped them, pinching her nipples, her head rolling from side to side. An erotic masterpiece, the hottest thing I ever saw, so hot my cock dripped precum onto the sheet under me.

I doubled my efforts, lapping up to her clit and flicking the sensitive nub, driving my fingers in and out of her heat. "Oh God... *fuck,* Spencer... don't stop... r-right there, I'm... I'm..."

I rode it out with her, holding on when she threatened to buck me off as her body took over. She howled, gripping the pillow under her head, straining before falling back with a deep sigh.

I did that to her.

There was no satisfaction sweeter.

"Is there anything else I can do for you this morning?" I kissed my way up and down her inner thighs, chafing the delicate skin with my morning stubble.

A soft smile touched her mouth as her eyes fluttered open. "That depends. What did you have in mind?" she asked in a soft, playful voice.

"I was thinking..." Reaching across the bed into the nightstand, I retrieved a condom. "I should sink my cock deep inside this pretty pussy and fuck the hell out of you."

Desire flashed in her eyes, and she bit her lip, nodding. "I think that sounds like a very good idea."

With the latex rolled down my length, I parted her thighs and positioned myself between them. "You want my cock, sweetheart?"

"Want, need, what's the difference?" she asked, locking her legs behind my back.

Fuck, how was she so perfect? Not only her body, which I would never get tired of, but the woman she was inside. There was no awkwardness, no shame in announcing what she wanted. She didn't play coy, didn't pretend her libido was just as strong as mine. I didn't know until now what a fucking turn-on that was. She had taught me more than she could ever understand.

Rowan gasped softly when I breached her entrance, filling her in one sure stroke. Her mouth fell open, and her back arched while a low moan vibrated in her throat. "You feel so good," she whispered, moving with me, meeting me stroke for stroke, taking me the way I took her. It was intoxicating.

I realized as I leaned down to kiss her that I wanted to do this every morning. Every night. I wanted to fall asleep next to her the way I had after dinner and hours of conversation last night. I wanted to wake up and indulge in her every morning.

I wanted *us*.

"Harder," she whispered, eyes meeting mine, staring into my soul. "Fuck me."

She gasped when I gave her what she wanted, driving deep, hard, rocking my bed in a rhythm that quickened as we both got swept up in the moment. In each other. Her moans echoed around us, the sound adding to the inferno building. Her nails dug into my ass, pulling me deeper, and it was almost enough to make me lose control.

Not yet.

But I was losing my grip, pushed closer to the edge with every stroke, every time she moaned my name. "Spencer... fuck..."

Caught between relief and disappointment when she clenched around me, signaling the end, I wanted more, even though this couldn't last forever. But there would be more. There had to be. Giving this up wasn't an option.

That thought was still at the forefront when I had no choice but to grit my teeth and give in to the sensation rushing through my body. My balls pulled up, and I came until my ears rang, then collapsed in a heap at her side. She was splayed out on the bed, breathless, glowing in the morning sun. I would've given anything to freeze this moment. To live in it forever.

Fuck, was this love? It didn't matter how I tried to fight it. There was never any hope.

When she sighed heavily, I almost believed she'd heard my thoughts and was reacting. Instead, she opened her eyes and groaned. "I really need to get moving. I have to go home and get ready for work."

"Take a day off," I suggested, but she only laughed.

"Would you mind if I take a shower first?" When I arched an eyebrow, she shook her head. "No, that is not an invitation. I really do need to move my ass, and something tells me you're not going to help things."

"Are you kidding? I'll wash your back while you take care of the front. You will get done in half the time."

"Yes, because I'm sure it would be that easy." When I reached out, hoping to grab hold of her, she managed to escape my clutches and roll out of bed. I took in the sight of her glorious ass as she ducked into the bathroom and closed the door.

As much as I would've liked to spend the rest of the day doing exactly what we had just finished, she had a point. We both needed to get on with our lives. It was so easy to escape back to this world we were creating together, even if neither of us meant to do it. Whenever it was the two or three of us, if Hannah was around, there was no one else in existence. Only us. And somehow, that was enough.

Who am I turning into?

All I knew was I could never be the man I was before.

For the first time in as long as I could remember, I had left my phone in my pants pocket instead of making sure to place it on the nightstand where I could easily reach it. Nothing had mattered more than getting her out of her clothes and taking her. Now, I got up, running my hands through my hair to smooth it a little while looking around for my pants. I found them kicked halfway under the bed and reached down to pull the phone free.

That was when I discovered my mistake. I should've been paying attention to the phone.

Bruce: *Call me immediately.*

Connor: *Jesus Christ, call me when you see this.*

Lex: *What the fuck is this story about you? Is it true? How the hell did I not know?*

That was only the beginning. There were so many more texts and missed calls. A sense of the world coming to an end gripped me, even as the sound of Rowan's soft humming in the shower filled the air. It wasn't. It couldn't be.

She wouldn't...

All it took was opening the text app and clicking the link Lex had sent. The headline was a punch in the gut that took my knees out from under me, making me drop to the bed while I stared in disbelief at the ugly accusation.

Ugly because it was true.

Tech Guru Guilty of Destroying Actress's Career

I struggled to skim the first few lines of the story, every word making my blood run colder—*Spencer Collins' reckless driving caused a brutal car crash, which left his pregnant girlfriend permanently disfigured... fled the country while her family was forced to raise the daughter he refused to acknowledge.*

No. Anything but this. I was going to be sick. My stomach churned, and I was sure whatever was left in there would come out all over me and my phone and everything else. It wasn't possible. Yet there it was, in front of me. The deepest betrayal. A knife to the heart.

It had to be somebody else.

Amazing, the way I immediately jumped to defend her. I didn't want to believe it, but who else could it have been? Few people knew about the crash, but even fewer knew about Hannah and the circumstances she grew up in.

Disappointment crashed into me, stole the air from my lungs, and left me shaking. This was a woman I thought I would want for the rest of my life, and all the time, she had planned on betraying me this way. There was no other explanation. Unless Dad did it to get back at me somehow, but why would he? It would mean implicating himself in the cover-up.

I stood when the bathroom door opened, my back to her when she emerged. "That water pressure is insane," she reported with a happy sigh. "What I wouldn't give to have that at my place."

Even now, she pretended. My blood was boiling, my heart was pounding, and bile was rushing into my throat. She was the only one who could've done it—he only one with a reason to get back at me.

"I hope you're proud of yourself," I growled, turning toward her, watching her eyes widen as she stopped in the middle of running a towel over her body.

"Excuse me?" She had the nerve to let out a disbelieving laugh as she looked behind her like she was searching for whoever I must be talking to.

"What did I do wrong now? I wasn't even in the bathroom for long."

I pitched the phone across the bed, watching as it landed in front of her. She looked down at it, then up at me, her features pulled together in confusion.

How could she do it?

How could she act like this?

I could count on one hand the number of people who knew about that night, all of whom had something to lose by exposing me, except for her, so long as she managed to keep her name out of it and deny breaking the contract she signed. It had to be her, no matter how much part of me wanted to believe otherwise.

"Read it," I grunted. "And congratulate yourself. You fucked me over. You finally got the last punch. The death blow."

"What the hell are you talking about?" She was laughing, but it was tense, nervous laughter. I would've been nervous in her position. Knowing I got caught.

Through my teeth, I grunted, *"Read. It."* It was like I had never seen her before. I was staring at a stranger, one with the ability to lie to my face and not give two shits.

How could she?

It had all been a lie from the beginning.

She huffed but picked up the phone, shaking her head before she began to read.

Then the phone started to shake. "No," she breathed out, eyes widening by the moment. Her mouth fell open, lips peeling back from her teeth in an expression of horror.

"What? Did you think he wouldn't go public? That he wouldn't contact every fucking tabloid in existence that wasn't owned by the Diamond family?" Because, of course, Connor would never allow something like this in one of his publications. But there were plenty of others, no matter how vast the family empire happened to be.

"No. *I didn't!*" She dropped the phone on the bed, lifted her head, and stared at me from across the sheets we had tangled what felt like a lifetime ago but was only minutes. Incredible how everything changed all at once. I was staring at a stranger now.

"No?" I barked out a laugh while pulling on a pair of sweatpants. "What a fucking joke. That's all you can think to say? No?"

"What do you expect me to say?" A glance her way told me she was shivering, crossing her arms over her bare tits, following my every move. "I had nothing to do with that. Spencer, I *would never!*"

"Bullshit!" I shouted, the sound loud and sharp enough to make her jump. Good. Let her be afraid. She should've been. "You were the only other person who knew about Hannah, right? How your parents raised her after I ran off." The more I thought about it, the more obvious it was. "I sure as fuck never told anybody what happened except my business partner, and he wouldn't sabotage us like this."

I laughed in complete disgust at the woman I imagined making a life with only ten minutes ago. "What, it wasn't enough?" I demanded while tears welled in her eyes. They wouldn't help. "Your great career, your promising future, the life you swear you're so satisfied with? It wasn't enough that I apologized and told you I never meant to desert you?"

Holding up a hand so she wouldn't say another word, I asked, "Or did you spill your secrets to Damian before the night I thought we cleared the air? I haven't forgotten how hostile you were when we first reconnected. What did he offer? Money? Or was the chance to destroy my name enough for you?"

"I already told you." Now, anger leaked into her voice. It wasn't so shaky and weak. "I didn't do it. This wasn't me!"

"Who the fuck was it? Tell me. If it wasn't you,

who could it have been?" I wanted her to tell me. I needed her to. I needed to believe there was another explanation because I didn't know if I could live with myself otherwise.

When the best she did was whimper, my heart hardened for good. I snarled, "Get your shit together, walk out the door, and make sure I never have to look at you again. I've got much more important things to handle now that you've completely fucked my life."

"Spencer." Her voice quivered. "Please. Don't do this. I'm telling the truth. Why won't you listen to me?"

"I'm done listening to you. Consider the scales balanced. Congratulations." I picked up her dress that was on the floor at the foot of the bed and picked it up, throwing it in her direction. "Get dressed and get the fuck out of here. Now!" I barked when she didn't move fast enough.

"But what about Hannah?"

Hannah. Her name made me second-guess everything that had come out of my mouth, but I hardened my heart. "I'm not giving her up. You'll hear from my lawyer. We'll make arrangements that way." This was too fucking much. I couldn't handle it in front of her. I needed to be alone, where I couldn't see her or hear her voice. It was bad enough I smelled her all over me.

"So that's it?" she whispered. "You won't give me a chance to defend myself? You won't even listen? That's how this ends?"

"No. That's not how this ends because there was never anything to end." That much was obvious, no matter how the words choked me. How was there anything real between us if she could commit a betrayal like this?

The phone on the bed buzzed, reminding me of what I had in store—phone calls, demands, accusations. No doubt Miles would call, frantic, pissed off. I couldn't blame him. I'd assured him I had this under control.

Then, I had to go and lose sight of the ball. Too busy playing house, pretending to be a family, trying to make up for my father's callousness and cruelty.

What a joke. Because of that, here I was, watching my life fall apart while a sniffling, whimpering woman pulled on her clothes. The phone buzzed again, and I turned away from it, pulling back the curtain and gazing out over yet another perfect day. Not so perfect from where I was standing.

"Would you at least let me speak? Because—"

"So help me, God, Rowan," I growled out, gripping the windowsill until my hands ached. "I'm not going to say it again without screaming. You need to go, and you need to make sure I do not see you again. Everything can be handled between our lawyers. I guess you'd better find one."

"It. Wasn't. Me. You're going to regret this," she whispered, footsteps heading for the bedroom door. "You stupid prick. You're going to feel so sorry when you realize what you lost. I guess it's easier for you this way. You can run away again without looking like a coward."

"I told you to get the fuck out of my apartment!" It only felt good in the moment, screaming that way, bellowing out my rage, disappointment, and betrayal. Letting it all out only left room for other things to fill the void. Regret was the big one.

That got her moving, anyway. The next thing I heard was the slamming of my front door. I closed my eyes and drew a deep, shaky breath, fighting to control my nervous system before the panic and rage built to the point where I couldn't contain them anymore.

There would be a way out of this. There had to be. Damage control—threatened lawsuits against the publications who ran the story. They couldn't possibly have proof. I'd have someone read the articles for me since I doubt I could do it myself. Not without losing what little group I had on myself.

Behind me, the phone buzzed and buzzed. Instead of picking it up and opening Pandora's box, I gave myself another minute to breathe. To grieve the fantasy I'd believed was real.

18

ROWAN

"Mom?"

"Hmm?" I looked down at my daughter, nestled against me on the porch swing. Her feet tucked up beside her, her book forgotten in my lap. I had lost track of how long we sat there together, with me rocking slowly, lost in my head.

"Are you ever going to go back to work?"

I had to chuckle even though my heart wasn't in it. She had a way of getting right to the point. "Of course I will. Just not quite yet."

"But it's been, like, a week. Hasn't it?"

Eleven days counting the weekends, but who was counting? I hadn't been to the office since the

Wednesday of my last dinner with Spencer. By now, the flowers were dead, along with everything else.

"People are allowed to take time off, you know." I rocked the swing, wishing the motion would soothe me. "Everything will be fine. I'm still checking in with the office every day. Noelle knows she can reach me if there are any problems. I just... I need this time."

"I'm sorry you're sad." Her head touched my shoulder again. "I wish I could make you happy."

That was the most painful thing of all, hearing her say that. "I know how you feel because I always want to make you happy when you're sad. But sometimes, there's nothing you can do. Like right now, I have to get through my sad feelings and get back to life. And I will," I promised. I just wish I knew how.

"Did you and Spencer break up?"

My God, she was determined to kill me. That was how it felt as I struggled to find the words. You couldn't break up what had never started, but that wouldn't help things. Instead, I told her the only thing I knew was true. "No matter what happens between me and Spencer, it won't change how we feel about you. He's not going anywhere." Hell, he had even kept the bodyguards watching the house and the school.

"Yeah, but what about you? If he makes you sad—"

"You have nothing to worry about," I insisted, cutting her off before her sweetness made me sob. I had done enough of that. "It's grown-up stuff. I know you don't want to hear that, but it's the truth. Everything will be okay in the end. I know that for sure."

I checked the time on my phone. "Why don't you go inside and get washed up for dinner? Maybe Grandmom needs a little help getting things together."

"You can tell me you want to be alone. It's fine." She kissed my cheek, hopping off the swing and heading inside. "I'll let you know when it's time to eat."

It was starting to look more and more like I was the child and she was the parent. I needed a little parenting, hence my reason for hiding out at Mom and Dad's ever since that nightmare at Spencer's last Thursday morning.

Nothing had changed in the ten days after. I had heard nothing from him. I followed the story online, the accusations that had been hurled at him. None of them mentioned me by name, which, of course, came as a relief, not for myself, but for Hannah. She already knew too much. She was too young for the specifics.

I had asked Mom and Dad right away if they had told anyone what I confessed. "You never told us his last name," she'd reminded me. "How could we have gone to the press? And why would we?" She had looked so sad, so pained, the way I would if it was Hannah going through hell. "We wouldn't hurt you that way, and we would never hurt Hannah."

No, but sometimes things like this happened without a person realizing the toll it would take. That was why, instead of going inside, I waited on the porch for the person I knew would be joining us for dinner tonight at my invitation.

My phone read five forty-five when a familiar hatchback pulled up at the curb. I watched my sister climb out from behind the wheel. She noticed me right away. *Did her steps falter?* It looked that way, but then I might have been making it up in my head. Eventually, she reached the porch, eyeing me warily from the other end.

I had spent days mulling this over. Imagining all the things I would say to her. I had rehearsed this moment more thoroughly than I had ever rehearsed for a role. Yet, having her in front of me was a different story. All that flew out of my head, leaving behind the first thing that came to mind. "I hope you're proud of yourself."

Rhiannon blinked rapidly, her head snapping back. "Hi to you, too," she muttered, looking me up and down. "You look like hell."

I gave her the same up-and-down look, replying, "You're not looking so great, yourself. What happened to all the fancy clothes?" She was dressed the way I was used to seeing her, in an old band T-shirt and a pair of jeans with the knees ripped out. Almost like she had been pretending to be some-body else, wearing a costume. It was a well-fitting costume, but eventually, everybody got tired of pretending to be something they weren't.

"Uh... thanks?" She crossed an arm over herself, gripping her other elbow. That was always what she did when she felt exposed or nervous. "How are you feeling? Are you sick?"

"Can we please stop this? Because you know damn well how I'm feeling. You know I'm not sick, even if I sort of feel that way. Don't pretend Mom didn't already tell you why I've been here. I know that's why you've been steering clear. If this were any other situation, you would have been here by now."

"I don't know what you're talking about," she insisted with a nervous laugh. Her gaze kept sliding toward the front door like that was her way out. Her chance at freedom.

"Give it some thought," I suggested, slowly rocking the swing. "Maybe you'll remember. You know, you never did tell me the name of the man you were seeing. Why don't you tell me now?"

"Wow. You're giving me whiplash." She laughed. She could laugh all she wanted, but I saw the strain on her face, in her eyes.

"I'm curious. What's his name? What does he do for a living?"

"It doesn't matter. We are... not seeing each other anymore. That's over." Her brows drew together as her gaze dropped to the wood floor under us. She scuffed one of the planks with the toe of her sneaker. "He wasn't right for me."

"Because he's a goddamn sociopath?" I guessed, snickering when her head snapped up, eyes wide. "You know what, I'm feeling psychic today. Let me take a guess. Is his name Damian Fields?"

Her mouth fell open. Her mouth snapped shut. "See?" I muttered. "That's the one thing I was curious about. Would he use his real name? At first, I thought no, of course not. He would want to fly under the radar. But then I gave it some more thought and realized no, he would want us to know it was him pulling the strings all along. So how did he do it?" I asked, which in and of itself was a miracle seeing as how my heart was breaking, and stringing words together was becoming more and more challenging.

"Please." She hung her head again, shoulders rising and falling in a sigh. "Please, don't do this."

"Don't do what? Don't hold you accountable for something you've done?" I didn't want to scream out here in the open, so I settled for grunting out, "Dammit, Rhiannon. How could you? I know you hate Spencer, but he is Hannah's father, and you still went out of your way to hurt him."

She flinched. "Is that what you think happened? That I wanted revenge or something?"

"Don't tell me that had nothing to do with it."

"No. It didn't." She ran a hand under her eyes, sniffling now that she had given up the act. She was trembling, her body sagging before she perched on the railing running the length of the porch. "I swear. I didn't realize... I didn't know."

"Didn't realize what? That there was something strange about a guy you were seeing wanting to know about my past?"

"Just let me explain."

It was the funniest thing. My instinct was to say

no, to shut her down, to tune her out. Then again, that was what Spencer did to me. He wouldn't let me tell my side of the story, and I still resented the hell out of him for it. Now I understood how easy it was to stick my fingers in my ears, close my eyes, and pretend I couldn't hear anything that didn't fit within the narrative I had already constructed.

She must have taken my silence for acceptance because she continued in a soft voice, "Do you know how long it was since I felt... noticed? Special? The men I work with, they sit glued to their computers all day. They barely notice anyone or anything around them. And they have the social skills of toad-stools. You know how hard it is for me to meet people. I get three sentences in, and I say something stupid or nerdy or, I don't know." Lifting a shoulder, she concluded, "Whatever it is, it turns people off. But not him. He liked me, or he pretended to. He made me feel... pretty."

"For God's sake, Ree, you are pretty. You've always been pretty. Is that all it takes to make you spill a secret like that? Telling you you're pretty?" I was almost shouting and had to cut myself off before I got much louder.

"Oh, spare me the sanctimonious crap," she spat. Now, my head snapped back in shock. I could count on one hand the number of times she took that tone with me. Bright color flooded her cheeks, and her lip curled in a smear. "Look at you. You've had your entire life handed to you while some of us had to scratch and fight for every goddamn good thing that ever happened. For once, something good happened to me. For once, somebody saw me. Noticed me. Not the beautiful and perfect Rowan."

"Don't make this about that," I whispered, shaking my head. I didn't know whether to be sad, disappointed, or sickened by her excuses.

"But that's what it was about, don't you see? I wasn't trying to hurt anybody," she insisted, shaking her head fiercely. "I swear to God. Do you understand how stupid I feel? He used me. Looking back, I see it so clearly."

She scoffed and sneered again, though something told me she sneered at herself. "The questions he would ask about the family. Asking if I was close with you. What it was like growing up together. I thought, *wow*." She released a sigh, leaning against the post beside her. "Wow, he really wants to know about me. My life, my history. I told him all about Hannah, about helping raise her. Of course, he wanted to know why you weren't the one doing it. I walked right into his trap."

I was starting to understand. How he found her, I didn't know and might never, but at least I was starting to see how it all came together. It wasn't like she went out and sought him. "So, you told him everything," I concluded. "You hardly knew him. Why would you trust him with something like that?"

"I told you. He made me feel special. I honestly thought..." She covered her face with her hands. "I thought maybe this was it."

"Jesus..." I whispered.

"You don't get it!" Her hands dropped to her lap, tears flowing down her cheeks. "All our lives, it's always been about you. Rowan, the star. Beautiful, perfect Rowan. Everybody paid attention to you. I was always an afterthought. And then, what happened? You started dating this ridiculously wealthy guy, and he almost got you killed. You found out you were pregnant with his baby. Your face was disfigured, your career went up in smoke. And then what happened?"

She barked out a brutal laugh that chilled my blood. "You somehow managed to pivot and ended up doing better than ever! Mom and Dad gave you everything. They let you come back home. They raised your baby for you so you could go to school. Because it's always about *you!* What's best for

Rowan. How can we help Rowan? Poor, tragic girl whose dreams were broken. What about *my* dreams? When did anybody give a shit about my dreams?"

She scoffed, either at me or herself, standing and turning around to gaze out over the street. "I finally had something for me, and I was so desperate and so lonely, I walked straight into it. What an absolute joke."

I had known that, hadn't I? That she felt overshadowed. All the photos in the living room, the way our parents had always bragged about me while rarely doing the same over her. How awkward she felt around people. How rare it was for her to leave her shell.

One day, I might find it in me to feel sorry for her. This was not that day, not with my battered heart still struggling to beat. Not when the pain of losing Spencer again was so fresh and sharp.

"When did he approach you? I need to know," I told her when she snorted. "I need to put it together in my head, for myself."

"I don't know." Her head tipped back, and she heaved another sigh. "The day before you went out on that date. I assume it was with Spencer."

"The night of the break-in?"

"Right. We met the night before that. I went to

my usual place to pick up dinner on my way home. He was behind me in line and struck up a conversation over whether he should get a chicken cutlet sandwich or meatball parm. We ended up having dinner together at the restaurant. It all sort of snowballed after that."

This meant it was the night after Spencer and I found each other at the award luncheon, then went for drinks in the evening. Was he following Spencer around all this time? More likely, he had someone else doing his dirty work. Probably more determined than ever to dig up dirt on him.

Spencer visited my office the next afternoon, didn't he? Asked me out. With all of Damian's money and all of his ruthlessness, I didn't doubt it was child's play, dredging up more information about my family and me after confirming our association. Following my sister. He had the resources to find out just about anything on anyone. He would have known she was single.

Now I understood something else that had never occurred to me with so much bullshit drama threatening to drown me. Damian had probably sent that guy to the apartment to break in, to shake me up at the very least. Maybe to find more information on Spencer.

"Honestly," she whispered, sliding a pleading look my way. "I wasn't trying to hurt anybody. Not you, not even Spencer, definitely not Hannah."

I wasn't trying to hear that. Not with a hurricane raging inside me. "So you told him about the accident," I concluded.

She gulped, nodding. "Vaguely. I swear to God. I told him it was some rich guy named Spencer."

That was all he needed to know. Some rich guy named Spencer had crashed his car with me inside and gotten away unscathed. "You told him Spencer was Hannah's father," I added, groaning when she nodded in response. "You told him I wanted to be an actress?"

"There were so many conversations. It's not like I told him everything at once." Now she was defensive, shoulders hunched, eyes hard. "Yes, I must have."

Chilly silence unfurled between us and hung in the air for a long time. My heart was too heavy. I didn't know what to say. I didn't know how to feel about her. "I'm going to need time with this," I decided, standing and heading for the door. "If you're going to be here, fine. I'll be up in the bedroom."

"Wait, Rowan," she pleaded with tears in her voice. "Please, don't hate me."

I didn't know how I felt, whether I hated her or not. I only knew I couldn't say another word without either screaming or sobbing. It was better to remove myself from the situation, so I headed inside and straight upstairs without another word. She could explain my absence to Mom and Dad.

19

SPENCER

"If there's one surefire way to make the public forget bad press, it's introducing something even worse." My cousin Connor laughed somewhere on the East Coast, and I could hear ice tinkling in his glass like he was enjoying a celebratory drink.

After nearly two weeks of slugging it out in the mud, I was ready to join him.

"This should put an end to it," he predicted. "I knew for sure once we found those two employees Fields poached from you, we would have it made."

I sat in front of my open MacBook, checking out one headline after another. *Tech guru accused of sabotage and competition. Tech genius poached competitor employees to steal secrets. Tech golden boy used arson, sabotage, bribery to get ahead.*

Miles was the third party on our conference call, and he released a huge sigh. "We have one thing he couldn't get his hands on. Proof."

He was right. Proof in the form of signed testimonials describing the tactics Damian used to lure employees out of my company and into his. The promises he made, money he wired to their bank accounts through shell companies. He was generally smart enough not to leave a paper trail, but they did. They'd provided printouts of emails they sent him, screenshots of text messages, all of which pointed to very dirty dealings.

The second Connor ran the story this past weekend, the world forgot about me. There was no proof of anything printed about Rowan, whose name was never mentioned, and me. As much as I loathed Damian, I had to give him credit. He knew better than to drag anyone else's name into this since they could easily sue. No doubt Rowan warned him about that. She wouldn't want that sort of publicity around her.

In other words, there was no real story outside of unsubstantiated, secondhand rumors. A couple of phone calls to our respective Board members had helped soothe their concerns. Once we presented them with the proof Connor's investigator pulled together, we were home free.

Since then, one of his thugs must have figured it was a good move to go to the authorities. He lawyered up, ready to talk about certain illegal activities in East Hampton and Silicon Valley, including a recent break-in at a competitor's offices.

"Stupid sons of bitches like him never stop while they're ahead," Connor concluded with a dry laugh. "Enough is never enough. They get away with something small, so they decide to go bigger, until finally, they become so brazen it's inevitable that they're caught. I'm only glad I was able to be part of this."

"I can't thank you enough, cousin. Really. The same for Lucian and Ivy," I added, thinking about the amount of effort the two co-directors of the company's digital media team had put into their social media campaigns. "You've been lifesavers." I meant every word and so much more I couldn't verbalize. The problem was, I felt none of it. I knew I should, that eventually I might, but not then. Not in my otherwise empty apartment surrounded by what I used to consider solitude but now felt more like loneliness once the call ended.

I should've been celebrating. That motherfucker

was going down. There was nothing standing in the way of our patent's approval. We were about to usher in a new era, Miles and me. I should've called my friends to see if they would have a drink with me, maybe catch dinner. There was plenty to catch up on.

I couldn't bring myself to do any of it. I didn't have it in me to listen to ball-busting and guy talk, either.

I came so close to having everything I never knew I wanted or needed. Life would have been easier and simpler if I had never met my daughter.

I wouldn't turn my back on her. That much I knew for sure. My lawyer had already reached out to Rowan, and as far as I knew, we were waiting for her to make a move when it came to discussing visitation. I wouldn't demand custody and put Hannah through that. I was willing to settle for getting to know each other better for now. Of course, that meant telling her I was her father, but she would find out eventually.

I settled back on the sofa, staring at the ceiling. A king in his castle. What the fuck did it get me at a time like this when I couldn't shake the feeling of losing something I never had? It was my stupid fault for caring as much as I did, letting myself get close to them. I hated that Hannah had to be any part of this, but then I wasn't the one who decided to talk to the enemy. That was all on Rowan.

The worst part was none of it made a difference for Damian. Not in any positive way. He had dug his own grave by kicking the hornet's nest, and Rowan had helped him do it. At least he was out of our way for good, even if it meant sacrificing...

Nothing. I had sacrificed nothing because I had nothing. She was a woman I fucked. Somebody I'd spent time with. It didn't have to be anything more than that. I would move on like I had previously. We would sure as hell be busy once the patent was approved, and I had already taken the extra steps to have the application expedited. There would be more than enough to distract me.

But this wasn't like before. There was no trip to China in my immediate future. I wasn't trying to forget a terrible mistake and the fallout that resulted. I couldn't talk myself into forgetting the very real feelings that had bloomed in me and were now withered.

I was tempted to ignore my phone when it rang. Anyone who needed me at nine on a Monday night could wait. The ringing stopped, and I closed my eyes, soaking in the silence until it rang again.

Blowing out a sigh, I sat up and looked down at where the phone sat on the table.

Hannah.

I picked up without thinking, at least a dozen ugly scenarios racing through my head in the time it took me to answer the call and say, "Hello?"

"Hi," she said. "Um... you told me I could call whenever I wanted."

The sound of her voice turned my throat into a pinhole. I barely sucked in a breath at first, but I was able to reply, "Yes, of course. I'm glad you called. How are you? Wait. It's a school night. You're up pretty late."

"I know, I know. I couldn't sleep."

"Why not?" I asked. "Something bothering you?"

"Yeah, actually." She sounded nervous, poor kid. "I just wanted to ask if you're still mad at Mom."

She may as well have punched me. "Did she ask you to call?" I asked, suspicious.

"Oh no!" The way she said it told me it was the truth. "She would kill me if she knew I called you. Please, please don't tell her. She would never let me use the phone again."

A little dramatic, but somehow, I believed her. "Who said I'm mad at your mom?"

Her heavy sigh was enough to make me grin

despite the situation. "Why does everybody always treat me like a baby? I'm not stupid. I can see things. I hear things. Jeez. Like…"

I waited a beat before prompting. "Like what?"

"I wasn't supposed to tell you I know this, but… I know you're my dad. I figured it out," she blurted out a second later. "I mean, you're like the only guy Mom has ever introduced me to that she was, like, dating or whatever. And you were so nice to me. And we kind of look alike," she added.

It was out. She didn't sound disappointed, which I took as a good sign. "But your mom told you to pretend you didn't know?"

"She said it would be nicer if you told me your-self. But this is an emergency. So I didn't want to wait."

The use of the word emergency made the hair rise on the back of my neck. "What's happening? You can tell me."

"Okay, don't get mad at me or anything, and maybe don't tell Mom…"

"Hannah…" I sighed.

"Last night, she was fighting with Aunt Ree out on the front porch at Grandmom and Granddad's house. I wasn't supposed to be listening, but I couldn't help it."

I was torn between wanting to chide her the way I knew I should have and demanding to hear more. "I'll overlook that for now."

"Aunt Ree did something bad," she whispered. "Mom was really mad at her. Something about a guy she was going out with and how he tricked her. Aunt Ree told him stuff she wasn't supposed to. Like that, you're my dad. Something about an accident. That was all I could hear, really. Grandmom came in, and I had to pretend I wasn't listening..." She paused, adding, "Then Mom cried all night. She was supposed to go back to her apartment after dinner, but she stayed here instead and went home this morning. She was too upset last night."

Déjà vu. Once again, I was left weak by a sudden revelation. Instead of finding my name slandered in the press, I was facing down my own stupid, knee-jerk reaction. "You're sure that's what you heard?" I asked, my head spinning, my pulse racing.

"And Mom is so sad," she continued. "That's why I called. I was with her every day last week, and she just kind of sat there. She tried to be happy, but she couldn't. And I heard her crying all the time. Please, don't tell her I told you," she added in a rush. "I don't want her to be embarrassed or anything."

"I promise," I assured her almost without thinking. It couldn't be true, could it? Why would she lie?

Just when I thought she couldn't break my heart more than she already had, she asked a question that threatened to tear it from my chest. "I didn't do anything wrong, did I?"

"Listen to me." If there was one thing I could get right, it was this. "You did nothing wrong. The things that are going on all started before you were born. From way back, a long time ago. You are an amazing, wonderful girl, and I am so glad to get to know you. No matter what happens between me and your mom, that's not going to change. I'm not going anywhere."

"Then how come I didn't see you for two weekends?"

Fuck. She was not making this easy. "You know what? You're right, it's unfair. I don't want to avoid you just because things are messy right now." That was the nicest way I thought to describe it.

"Why does it have to be messy? Can't you just make up?"

"Hannah, I'm going to tell you a secret. I messed up. I messed up really bad." Talk about the understatement of the century. I had single-handedly fucked up the best thing that ever happened to me. I should have let her try to explain. Why didn't I let her? I'd said unforgivable things. How could I ever make up for that?

"Are you still there?" Hannah asked.

"I'm still here. I'm not going anywhere." My thoughts were racing, ideas bouncing around inside my skull. "I have to find a way to make it right."

"What are you going to do?" There was excitement and hope in her voice. I loved hearing it even if I wasn't quite sure how to respond just yet.

"I'm going to figure it out," I decided, getting up from the couch and putting aside the depressed bum act I'd perfected over the past week or so. "And I think I'm going to need your help. Will you help me?"

Her gasp brought a genuine smile to my face. "Yeah! Just tell me what to do."

Out of the long list of mistakes I'd committed, pushing Rowan away had to sit near the top. I could only hope it wasn't too late to win her back.

20

ROWAN

"Mom! Hurry up!" Hannah skipped along a few steps ahead of me, somehow managing not to spill any of her popcorn out of the large bucket. How did I let her talk me into buying a large when it easily fed a family of four?

"Would you relax?" I asked, already exhausted by the almost manic energy she'd bombarded me with all day. "The movie doesn't start for another five minutes. And there's going to be twenty minutes of previews. I bet you." I had only reluctantly agreed to go to a movie Saturday afternoon after my first week back in the office. Not that I would ever let her see how reluctant I was. As far as she was concerned, I was starting to get back to my old self, though nothing was further from the truth.

She had always brought so much to my life and still did, but now there was a raw, aching hole where Spencer used to be. Before this, there was always the secret hope that one day he would come back to me. Now, I understood how long I had nurtured that fantasy without admitting it to myself. The possibility had always been there and had granted me strength in my darkest moments.

Where was I going to get that strength from now? I had to be strong for my girl. I would have to learn to be strong without hope burning in my chest.

Hannah held open the door to the theater at the end of the hall, one of a dozen in the multiplex where they were playing the latest superhero movie. She was starting to get into them, probably because the other kids in her class were as well. I was already in the theater and standing beside the back row when I realized something. "Why is it empty?" I whispered.

Why was I whispering? There was nobody here to hear me.

"I don't know. This is the time on the tickets." She showed them to me, and sure enough, we were in the right theater at the right time.

"We just got lucky. We get the whole theater to ourselves." Though I doubted it. Somebody else had to show up. Somebody who shared my belief that it didn't really make a difference how early you showed up to a movie, especially now that theaters like this one let us pick our seats in advance.

We were in one of the center rows, our seats toward the middle. "Now let's be careful with the popcorn," I warned, remembering the way she threw up after the last movie we went to. "Once we get halfway down this huge bucket, I'm going to set it aside for a little while."

"It was only a dollar more than the medium size," she reminded me, exasperated.

"And that's how they get you to spend more money." Wow. I was sounding more and more like my own parents every day. What a pleasant thought to add to the other pleasant thoughts I'd been entertaining all week.

It wasn't long before the lights went down, and the screen lit up. I settled in and prepared for two hours of mind-numbing explosions and CGI effects. Hannah vibrated with excitement in her seat. I had no idea these movies meant so much to her. Apparently, I needed to reacquaint myself with my daughter after weeks spent with my head in the clouds.

Instead of a *Coming Attractions* title card, the screen went white. Animated letters appeared against the background as if some invisible finger was writing them in an old-fashioned script.

Once upon a time...

I looked at Hannah, who didn't seem confused.

The letters dissolved, replaced by a two-dimensional animated girl with blonde hair and blue eyes who stood on a stage, illuminated by spotlights. A deep voice filled the air, coming from the speakers set up along the walls. "Once upon a time, there was a girl. Beautiful, talented, with big dreams."

I had to be imagining things. More than two weeks of broken sleep and stress cleaning had left me delirious. Maybe I had no business driving home because I would've sworn I was listening to Spencer.

The silhouetted audience sitting in front of the animated girl got on their feet and applauded, throwing roses onto the stage. "She moved to Hollywood and worked hard," the narrator continued as the background switched to one featuring the Hollywood sign.

This was starting to get weird. Again, I looked at

Hannah, but she could only stare at the screen, her eyes wide and shining. The picture changed, and now I was looking at a bustling club. People moved in silhouette, and voices overlapped in the background while music played. That blonde girl stood behind a bar, serving drinks.

"One night..." the narrator, who had no right to sound so much like Spencer, continued. "She met a boy." A male figure slid into the frame, leaning against the bar, looking smug. I couldn't believe it was a coincidence that he, too, had blond hair and blue eyes, much like Spencer.

"That boy was young and arrogant and full of himself, but he saw something special about the girl. She was beautiful and funny and kind. He felt like he had known her all his life."

Tears filled my eyes as a montage of quick, animated clips passed— two of them in a jet, flying over San Francisco Bay, one on the beach, where he tried to teach her to surf, and another eating ice cream on the Santa Monica Pier.

"It was all magic... until one night," the narrator continued in a darker, somber voice. "The boy made a mistake he would regret for the rest of his life. He was reckless and stupid and trying to show off for the girl he was in love with."

I tensed all over at the sight of a sports car zipping off into the distance. A tear rolled down my cheek.

The screen went dark, but the voice went on. "He tried so hard to find her after that, but other people got in the way. What he didn't know was the girl had a secret even she didn't know about until after they weren't together anymore."

A new image filled the screen, this time featuring a little baby with wispy, golden curls. I laughed through my tears.

"And after that, the beautiful, brave girl worked so hard to make a big life for her baby." Again, there was a montage of images—studying late at night, taking exams while bleary-eyed, graduating in a cap and gown, beaming from ear to ear.

Finally, cartoon Rowan stood tall and proud in a fitted suit, hands on her hips like a superhero. "She was incredible. She helped people. And when the boy who hurt her came back into her life, he knew one thing right away before he could admit it to himself."

Cartoon Spencer slid back into the frame, standing close with an arm around my cartoon waist. "He wanted to try again. To do it right this time. And when he found out about his beautiful, brilliant little girl, he knew he wanted them to be a family." Cartoon Hannah popped up in front of us, arms folded, smirking. It was incredibly adorable.

Through the tears blurring my vision, I watched a figure emerge from behind a curtain alongside the screen. Spencer held a microphone in one hand and a sheet of paper in the other. His script, I assumed. He dropped it, coming to a stop square in the center of the floor and looked up at me. "He messed up. He should have let her tell her side of the story. He was too hurt and confused, and he took it out on her. He should have known better than to think she would do anything to hurt him or anybody else. And he was so, so sorry. He would've done anything for another chance because he loved her. He had always loved her."

Nobody told me this movie would be a tear-jerker. I would've brought more tissues. Tears soaked into my T-shirt by the time I stood, holding onto the seat in front of me for dear life while I tried to process what to do next. What to say. How to feel.

"Mom?" Hannah stood beside me, nudging me gently. "This is the part where you forgive him."

She was right. This was the point in the script where I was supposed to profess my love and leave everything else behind. What a shame real life was more complicated.

He looked like he was holding his breath down there, eyes glued to me. Was it wrong that I wanted him to suffer a little? I couldn't forget the things he said. The way he said them. Furious, spiteful.

Now, he was a man whose life hung in the balance. He was hanging on to my every move. "Rowan?" he silently mouthed. "Please."

I could be spiteful too. Would it make me happy, though? Wasn't happiness better than balancing the scales? The man I loved was standing in front of me, and I loved him too much to spend another minute questioning myself.

My heart led me to him, out of the row, and down to where he stood waiting with his arms open. Jumping into them was both the scariest and most natural thing I could've done. Trusting him, forgiving him. There was no other choice because I loved him too. I always had.

"Can I assume this means I'm forgiven?" he whispered in my ear, squeezing me tight.

"You're forgiven," I whispered back, tightening my grip around his neck. "So long as you never *ever* speak to me like that again. I'm forgiving, but I'm not a doormat."

"I swear. Never again." His lips brushed my ear. "I am so sorry."

I believed him. This was the sort of happy ending I had dreamed about all my life. Only I wasn't acting it out for an audience.

Or was I? Applause rang out from the back of the theater. I looked up and shielded my eyes, trying to see who was up there. Mom and Dad waved, and so did my sister. We had exchanged dozens, maybe hundreds of text messages since Sunday, clearing the air and understanding each other better than we had before. She looked just as happy as our parents. Maybe even more so.

"How did you do this?" I asked, laughing and crying at the same time.

"It helps when your best friend owns a studio with an animation division. He owed me at least half a dozen favors," Spencer explained, chuckling. "But I made sure everybody got paid double. What do you think?"

"I think it's very sweet that our daughter now knows where she came from," I pointed out. "And I think I love you. No. I *know* I love you."

His gaze softened as he tucked a finger under my chin, raising it until we were eye-to-eye. "Thank God because I don't know what I would do if you didn't."

"Kiss!" Hannah squealed. "Aren't you going to kiss her?"

Once we finished laughing, I wound my arms around his neck. "One thing you're going to learn about her. She's impossible to say no to."

"Like her mother," he murmured, kissing me. It was soft and sweet, full of the promise of a future. Our future.

NORMALLY, I wouldn't have given up a Saturday night with Hannah for the world. But tonight, there was a lot of talking to do. Planning. Not to mention making up for lost time. So when Mom offered to take Hannah, giving us time alone together, I couldn't say no, especially when Hannah seemed so damn determined to send us on our way. Spencer promised to pick her up in the morning so we could go to breakfast. The simplest thing, yet it meant the world.

The day had started with me forcing myself out of bed, reminding myself that I owed it to my daughter to be present. Now, we were in the elevator up to Spencer's penthouse. I was holding the hand of the man I loved, a man who loved me, and this was the first day of the rest of our lives together. I had no doubt this was it.

This was real.

This was always.

It was clear from the second we were inside the apartment that conversation would have to wait. His hands were on me right away, pulling me close, running over my hips and ass as he lowered his head for a kiss so much deeper and hotter than the one we had exchanged in the theater. The sort of kiss that made my toes curl and my pussy moisten.

He picked me up, and I wrapped myself around him, lost in the kiss, lost in him as he stumbled his way through his living room and down the hall into the bedroom.

"Fuck, I've missed you," he grunted out, his body stretched out on top of mine once we reached the bed, his mouth doing unspeakable things to every inch of skin he found. I made it easier, unbuttoning my jeans between kisses and pushing them over my hips and down my thighs before pulling his polo shirt over his head so I could feast on the master-piece that was his chiseled body. For a long time, it was enough to explore each other, to kiss and caress. My body lit up with more than pleasure. It was pure joy. I was back where I belonged.

He worshiped me, honored me, kneeled between my legs, and slid away my panties before kissing a path up my thighs, spreading them. His deep, contented sigh made goose bumps pebble my skin. "How did I ever convince myself I could live without this?" he asked, slowly running the flat of his tongue over my slit.

Pretty soon, there was nothing I could do but close my eyes and give myself over to him, to this. The tip of his tongue flicked a quick rhythm against my clit, his throaty groans telling me how much he loved tasting me, making me roll my hips and grind against his face. He was right. I couldn't have lived without this.

"God, you're so damn good at this," I whispered, running my fingers through his hair while I held his head in place.

The heat built the way it always did. I trusted it and went with it, knowing Spencer wouldn't make me regret it. His tongue moved faster, his deep grunts vibrating through me. "Yes... don't stop, I'm gonna come..." My legs clenched around his head, and I squealed at the height of the wave before it crashed, and there was nothing but sweet, warm bliss. All of the tension of the past couple of weeks dissolved.

It wasn't enough. Only a drop in the bucket compared to how desperately I needed him. "Come here." I held my arms out, and he crawled up the length of my body, kissing me slowly as we continued undressing each other. I would never tire of his beauty, his firm muscles and strong arms that made me feel so safe.

That wasn't what was on my mind by the time he unrolled a condom and pulled me across the bed until my ass was on the edge. I squealed with laughter while he braced my legs against his chest, standing in front of me.

There was no laughing when he drove himself deep in one punishing thrust, almost without warning. I wasted no time using the leverage he had given me, pushing against his chest with my legs, fucking him while he fucked me. There would be plenty of time for making love. This was about giving ourselves what we'd both craved for too long. I knew it without the words being spoken, one of those things that didn't need to be said.

"F-fuck me... Spencer," I whispered, the words pouring out, my chest heaving, my body flushing, and my soul singing. Every nerve in my body was on fire, but it was a blaze I didn't want to extinguish. Not ever.

I was already halfway to another orgasm when he added a thumb to my clit, stroking it in time with the deep, hard strokes he delivered with his dick. "Fuck, that's good! Don't stop!" I whimpered. I was too happy. It felt too good. I thought we would never do this again.

"So damn tight... your pussy is squeezing me, ready to come for me..." he gritted out, his teeth clenched, grunting like a wild, dangerous animal. An animal who wanted nothing more than to slam himself into me until my legs shook and I sobbed his name.

It hit me like a speeding train, shattering me. "Spencer!" And then I couldn't hear anything over the blood roaring in my ears. Tears rolled down the sides of my face, but I was laughing, too, completely lost in emotions so intense I didn't know what to do with them. The floodgates opened, and there was no closing them, but it was good, so good.

He finished with a roar, and it was even better to curl up against him once he collapsed onto the bed. To feel his heart beating under my palm when I touched it to his chest. To listen as his breathing slowed the way mine did.

"Thank you," I whispered once I had regained the ability to speak without panting.

"For that? You never have to thank me for that." With an arm under his head, he smirked at me. "It's not like I don't get anything out of it."

"That's not what I meant," I told him, laughing softly. "Thank you for today. Thank you for going to all that effort to do something special."

"It was all Hannah's idea." When I arched an eyebrow, he shrugged. "I mean it. We brainstormed a few ideas, and she said something about happily ever after, just like in a movie."

"Wait. Are you serious? I thought you were joking!" I propped myself up on my elbow, staring at him in shock. "She helped you plan that?"

"She reached out to me earlier in the week and asked me when we were going to make up. You aren't supposed to know about that," he added, wincing.

"I guess I have her to thank too." The pieces were starting to come together and form the bigger picture. "I guess that's when you two shared the whole father-daughter thing?"

He nodded, his grin widening to a fond smile. "She's a miracle, that kid. Did we get lucky or what?"

The fact that he used the word we made tears fill my eyes again. I had done so much crying lately, but these were the kind I didn't mind shedding.

I didn't mind staying up through the night,

either, talking until dawn, planning, laughing, and dreaming about the future. I had spent such a long time dreaming alone.

I wouldn't be alone again. Not ever.

And that was the best gift anybody could ask for.

EPILOGUE
LEX

Ever since I was a kid, I've never wanted to do anything but make movies. Sure, I was raised around them. I'd witnessed meetings, phone calls, and screaming matches with temperamental directors. I had visited sets from a young age and had my illusions shattered, though it never lessened my fascination with the process—the magic of it.

Finding out my father was finally willing to give me a big-budget project of my own should have been a dream come true. The chance to prove myself. To show him I had what it took to manage the studio when the time came for him to step down as president.

I should have known there would be strings attached.

"Let me get this straight," I growled out. Coming to a stop in front of my father's desk, I tossed the contract his way. He looked down at it, wearing a smirk but didn't show any surprise. "You tell me I'm finally going to produce my first film. Yet I don't have any say in the script we chose. You already have a cast in mind and a list of agents to reach out to. And now, you tell me you've already chosen the director, and she's coming in to sign a contract I'm only looking at five minutes before she's due to arrive."

"Quite a succinct summation, Lex." My father folded his arms, wearing what was about to become a shit-eating grin. I had seen too many of them to think otherwise. "What are you so pissy about?"

"For starters, exactly what part of this project will have my fingerprints on it?" I demanded, throwing my hands into the air. My voice echoed in the spacious office. "Because so far, I've had nothing to do with it."

"Let's get this straight, here and now." His amused expression fell away before his face turned stony. "You know damn well what's at stake. The numbers are shit. There are fewer people buying movie tickets every month. Our streaming platform isn't worth the money we poured into it. We need a win, or else the studio is going to look a lot different this time next year."

He didn't need to explain what that meant. I'd already sat through meetings where ideas like partnering with another studio or selling off branding and merchandising rights on our biggest legacy franchises were discussed. Those ideas were never met with enthusiasm—pretty far from it. They were worst-case scenarios.

And they were looking more realistic all the time. "I get it," I said with a sigh as some of the fight drained out of me. "We don't want to take risks." He nodded slowly, and I added, "So why the hell give me a movie at all right now? If you don't trust me enough to make good—"

"Do us both a favor and get your personal feelings out of this." He stood, framed by the many awards, posters, and photos covering the wall at his back. If only the world knew the true Alexander Landry. They saw him as a humanitarian, a philanthropist, someone who happened to be born wealthy and influential and who now chose to use that influence to better the world around him.

He was also cold, demanding, and self-centered. Impossible to please. Crass and devoid of sentimentality. Granted, I'd inherited some of those qualities, but I didn't base my entire personality on them. "You'll make good because I've set it up, so success is inevitable. We're courting the hottest names in Hollywood... spending a shit ton of precious resources. You're the crown prince, and this is your first major project. That alone should help drum up enough interest to make this a hit at the box office."

"You're counting on everybody getting in line to see if I fail," I concluded. Strange how the realization did nothing to me. He had stopped surprising me a long time ago.

"I'm counting on you proving them wrong." Even his warmest smile landed flat and insincere. "You're going to produce the film that turns everything around."

Or else. He left that part out, not that it mattered.

"I wanted Erich Danvers directing this," I countered, making him groan and roll his eyes. "You know he's the smart choice. Hot as hell after his win at Cannes. Everybody wants a piece of him, and he was interested in working with the studio." I didn't bother mentioning the hoops I jumped through to court the guy and all for nothing. Dad would have laughed at me, chalked it up to hurt feelings.

"Ah, you know how it is." He wandered over to

the small refrigerator in the far corner and pulled out a bottle of sparkling water. I noticed he didn't bother offering one to me. "We have to be inclusive. Hire more women. We can't afford a whisper of scrutiny right now."

Because he failed to see the writing on the wall when the industry began to shift, it meant I had to accept some second-rate director with a shitty reputation around town. According to all sources, she was mercurial, stubborn to a fault, wouldn't give an inch when it came to her precious artistic vision. A pain in the ass I had no desire to work with.

A pain in the ass who marched into my dad's office like she was heading into battle. She wore a loose, flowing white dress and sandals, which slapped the floor with every determined step. Long, brown curls were piled high on her head and the thin, silver bracelets stacked on her wrist jangled when she lifted a hand to shake my father's. There were hoops on her ears, too, and at least half a dozen beaded necklaces hanging halfway down to her abdomen.

I swallowed hard, but it did nothing to wipe the sour taste from my mouth. An artsy bohemian. Exactly the sort of person I avoided like the plague.

The stench of incense had never much appealed to me.

"Summer Strawbridge," she announced, wearing a bright smile. "Thank you for this opportunity, Mr. Landry. I'm looking forward to working together."

Dad offered a patronizing, amused smile. "It's a pleasure, Miss Strawbridge, but you will be working with my son, Lex. He's taking the executive producer position on this film. I'm sure a pair of young people like yourselves will breathe new life into our studio."

It was like she hadn't noticed me until now. Her head turned, and bright, green eyes landed on me. Sized me up. Full lips tipped downward at the corners. "Lex." My name fell out of her mouth and landed with a thud while the air around us went cold. She was disappointed to be working with me rather than Dad. She took it as an insult. It was written all over the lines between her eyebrows, the furrowed forehead, the narrowed gaze. "I see."

"Summer," I murmured, sizing her up in response, not bothering to hide the disappointment, which was beginning to border on resentment at being forced to work with a notorious pain in the ass who thought she was too good to work with me.

What a shame the entire future of the studio rested on us playing nice.

NEED MORE?

Dive into this scorching bonus scene from *Scarred Heart* here:

https://dl.bookfunnel.com/gtz596d3cp

Enjoy x

BROKEN RULES

ELITE MEN OF LOS ANGELES BOOK 2

We have six months to make a movie—or destroy each other trying...

Lex

Producing my first major film was supposed to be my chance to prove I belong in this industry. Then Summer Strawbridge walked into my office, all sharp edges and unrelenting fire.

She's not the director I wanted, and I'm definitely not the producer she expected. Every meeting turns into a battle of wills. Every moment with her tests my patience... and my control. But there's no denying her vision—or the way she gets under my skin.

I can't decide if I want to kiss her or fire her.
   Maybe both.

But with six months to pull off the impossible, one thing's certain: we're either going to make the best movie of our lives... or we're going to destroy each other.

Summer

This was supposed to be my big break—a chance to prove I'm more than my past. But then I met Lex

Landry: nepo baby, arrogant prick, and annoyingly good-looking.

He doesn't respect me—or even like me—but we're stuck together. And as much as I hate it, he challenges me, sees me in ways no one else has.

I can't afford to fall for him. My career and pride are on the line. But every step with him feels like we're heading straight for disaster—and I'm not sure we'll survive the impact.

········

Available from all good bookstores and my website:

https://authormissywalker.com/collections/elite-men-of-los-angeles

ACKNOWLEDGMENTS

Writing a new series is always a bit of a challenge, but with the LA men, the idea just *clicked*. It felt like it was meant to be. Hollywood glitz and glamour has been in my blood since I was a kid—I used to sneakily read Jackie Collins novels under my dad's desk. She's the queen of all things sparkly and fabulous, after all.

I couldn't do this without my amazing beta team. Saskia, you're the Queen, always pushing and pulling me in the best ways possible—I adore you! Mumma Bear, your support is everything, as always. Karmin, your feedback is spot-on, and I love it.

To my dream team—Ella and Lauren—you make everything run smoothly behind the scenes so I can focus on writing. I literally owe you both the world. Thank you for making my life easier!

And to my readers, old and new—you all have my heart. Writing can be a lonely gig, and knowing I get to create a little escape for anyone who steps into my world is what keeps me going. I write because I love it, and I write to give your mind a chance to chill out for a bit. I hope you feel that little escape when you read my books!

Oh, and if you're craving a supportive, hilarious, and slightly smutty community, come join us over at Missy Walker's Book Babes on Facebook. It's the best place to laugh, chat, and lift each other up!

Stay fabulous.

Missy x

JOIN MISSY'S CLUB

Hear about exclusive book releases, teasers, discounts and book bundles before anyone else.

Sign up to Missy's newsletter here:
www.authormissywalker.com

Become part of Missy's Facebook Reader Group where we chat all things books, releases and of course fun giveaways!

https://www.facebook.com/groups/
missywalkersbookbabes

ABOUT THE AUTHOR

Missy is an Australian author who writes kissing books with equal parts angst and steam. Stories about billionaires, forbidden romance, and second chances roll around in her mind probably more than they ought to.

When she's not writing, she's taking care of her two daughters and doting husband and conjuring up her next saucy plot.

Inspired by the acreage she lives on, Missy regularly distracts herself by visiting her orchard, baking naughty but delicious foods, and socialising with her girl squad.

Then there's her overweight cat—Charlie, chickens, and border collie dog—Benji if she needed another excuse to pass the time.

If you like Missy Walker's books, consider leaving a review and following her here:

instagram.com/missywalkerauthor

facebook.com/AuthorMissyWalker

tiktok.com/@authormissywalker

bookbub.com/profile/missy-walker

ALSO BY MISSY WALKER

Elite men of Los Angeles

Scarred Heart

Broken Rules

Reluctantly Yours

Entangled Vow

Velvet Sin

Boundless Love

Elite Men of Manhattan

Forbidden Lust*

Forbidden Love*

Lost Love

Missing Love

Guarded Love

Infinite Love Novella

Elite Heirs of Manhattan

Seductive Hearts

Sweet Surrender

Sinful Desires

Silent Cravings

Sensual Games

Endless Love

ELITE MAFIA OF NEW YORK SERIES

Cruel Lust*

Stolen Love

Finding Love

SLATER SIBLINGS SERIES

Hungry Heart

Chained Heart

Iron Heart

SMALL TOWN DESIRES SERIES

Trusting the Rockstar

Trusting the Ex

Trusting the Player

*Forbidden Lust/Love are a duet and to be read in order.

*Cruel Lust is a trilogy and to be read in order

All other books are stand alones.